ALARCÓN

The Three-Cornered Hat

AND OTHER STORIES

TRANSLATED
AND WITH AN INTRODUCTION BY
MICHAEL ALPERT

PENGUIN BOOKS

Penguin Books Ltd, Harmondsworth, Middlesex, England
Penguin Books Inc., 7110 Ambassador Road, Baltimore, Maryland 21207, U.S.A.
Penguin Books Australia Ltd, Ringwood, Victoria, Australia
Penguin Books Canada Ltd, 41 Steelcase Road West, Markham, Ontario, Canada
Penguin Books (N.Z.) Ltd,
182–190 Wairau Road, Auckland 10, New Zealand

—

This translation first published 1975

—

Copyright © Michael Alpert, 1975

—

Made and printed in Great Britain
by Richard Clay (The Chaucer Press), Ltd,
Bungay, Suffolk
Set in Monotype Garamond

PEDRO ANTONIO DE ALARCÓN, the Spanish novelist, was born in Guadix in 1833. He first became popular for his eye-witness account of the Moroccan campaign of 1859, then for his impressionistic journal of a visit to Italy. His romantic short stories *Novelas Cortas* (collected 1881–2) deal with episodes in the Napoleonic Wars. His best-known work is *El sombrero de tres picos*.

MICHAEL ALPERT was born in London in 1935 and educated at the Polytechnic Secondary School and Downing College, Cambridge, where he read Modern Languages. Since 1964 he has been at the Polytechnic of Central London where he is now Senior Lecturer in Spanish. He holds a doctorate in Spanish history and is contiuning his research into the Spain of the 1930s.

His publications include a book of Spanish texts, a contribution to the translation of the *History of the Second World War* (fortnightly parts, 1973) and numerous commercial publications.

He has also translated *Two Spanish Picaresque Novels* for the Penguin Classics.

CONTENTS

INTRODUCTION

PEDRO ANTONIO DE ALARCÓN was born at Guadix in the province of Granada on 10 March 1833 and died on 19 July 1891. He came from a middle-class family impoverished by the turmoil of early nineteenth-century Spain. His father was obliged to send him to a seminary for his education because economic stringency did not permit his attendance at the law faculty of Granada University. However, he must have spent many hours in the cathedral, the chief glory of Guadix and, years later, wrote with passion of the impression it had made upon his youthful imagination.

He spent only a short time at the seminary before the religious Order which administered it was expelled by the anti-clerical action of the Government. As a result of the expulsion, Alarcón was able to collect the beginnings of a library from the dispersed volumes of the seminary. Determinedly, he set himself to learn French and Italian with the help of a Spanish and a French edition of Tasso's *Gerusalemme Liberata,* and an Italian translation of Virgil's *Aeneid.*

When Alarcón began to write, he established a literary paper called *El eco de occidente,* in partnership with a friend. The paper was edited from Guadix but published in the Atlantic seaport of Cádiz, where there were printers and literary circles. *El eco de occidente* appeared weekly and was dedicated to literature, the arts and the sciences. It was remarkably successful and ran for three years, for some of the time appearing in Granada. In it Alarcón published his early poetry and articles.

On 18 January 1853, just before his twentieth birthday, Alarcón arrived in Madrid where he tried in vain to establish himself as a poet. This disaster, and his summons for military service, obliged him to return home to Guadix. His parents, with a strenuous financial effort, managed to redeem him by the payment that allowed all but the poor to avoid service in the army.

Guadix had little more to offer Alarcón and he went to live in the provincial capital, Granada, in somewhat Bohemian style, continuing, however, to write for *El eco de occidente*. There, among the group of writers known collectively as the *Cuerda Granadina*, he began to establish his literary personality. He also developed political ideas, strongly espousing the centralizing, anti-clerical liberal causes embodied in the generals who led many of the palace *coups* of the time. As he writes in *The Three-Cornered Hat*:

'Poor Principle of Authority! How those of us who invoke you so often now treated you then!'

After General O'Donnell's successful Madrid *coup* of 1854, Alarcón led a rebellion in Granada, capturing the Town Hall and military headquarters. For a short time he edited *La redención*, a violently anti-clerical sheet.

Possibly circumstances impelled him to return to Madrid where he contributed to various news-sheets and in time became the editor of *El Látigo*, an intensely radical paper which advocated the overthrow of Queen Isabel II and the establishment of a republic. In 1855, perhaps as the result of a duel his over-violent articles had brought upon him, and disappointment with lack of support from his friends, he renounced political journalism and went to Paris on his first journey abroad, to cover the Industrial Exhibition.

In the same year he published his first novel, *El final de Norma*, written while recuperating in the quiet Castilian mountain town of Segovia.

The novel is a romance based on Bellini's opera and it is possible that the major disillusion that Alarcón experienced about this time and the change in his political and other attitudes, were responsible for his flowering as a novelist and in particular his decision to publish fiction based on his observations of Spain and Spanish life. On his return to

Madrid he found plenty of opportunity for journalism. He had become well known and connected: aristocratic salons and fashionable literary circles opened their doors to him. He wrote drama criticism, travel accounts and short stories, gathering material from visits to parts of Spain which he did not know, but especially from his native region.

Although Alarcón is not numbered among those nineteenth-century Spanish writers called *Costumbristas*, a category which included writers such as Mesonero Romanos and Estébanez Calderón with their scenes of Madrid or Andalusian life, and novelists who aimed at describing the life and customs of their city and telling their story only in second place, he nevertheless resembles them in basing his work on historical events and in places which he knew and with characters drawn from life. Basically, he was self-taught: he read and travelled widely and led a highly sociable life. He wrote for almost every literary paper in existence in Spain.

In 1859, influenced possibly by his friendship with General Ros de Olano, Alarcón enrolled in the army as a volunteer and went to fight in a colonial campaign in Morocco. The result was 'a bullet, two medals and a book'. This was his *Diario de un testigo de la guerra de Africa* (*Diary of a Witness of the War of Africa*). Alarcón defended the war and asserted that Spain had a natural field of colonial expansion in Morocco. His vision of military life was, however, highly idealized. The work was a huge success and Alarcón found himself a prosperous and well-known figure. He used some of his income from this work to take a six-months' vacation and travel through Spain, France, Switzerland and Italy as far as Naples, the record of which he published as *De Madrid a Nápoles* (1860). He observed closely, wrote eloquently of Italian art, and spoke to such famous figures of his time as Bellini, Cavour and Pope Pius IX. Much of his life was spent on these journeys which so often figure at the beginnings of his short stories, where his evident gift of sociability enabled him to collect many amusing anecdotes from older people who would willingly tell him their memories.

The publication of *De Madrid a Nápoles* was followed by a

pause in his literary production. Not until 1866 did he begin
to publish again, mostly collections of short stories, based
especially on the Peninsular War and the first Carlist War of
1833–9. Politics, in fact, had absorbed his attention and he sat
as a parliamentary representative for his home town of
Guadix, supporting the *Unión Liberal*.

One advantage of his political position was that he was able
to bring his younger brother, a priest in north-west Spain,
back to Guadix as a cathedral canon, where he would be able
to care for their widowed mother, their father having died in
1863.

In 1865, Alarcón married Paulina Contreras with whom he
lived a tranquil married life and had five children.

Politics brought him a short exile in Paris, followed by a
return to Granada. In 1868 he took part in the revolution
which overthrew the Bourbon monarchy. He was appointed
Minister Plenipotentiary to Norway and Sweden, but preferred to remain in Spain.

After observing the chaos of the years 1868–74, with an
invited king, Amedeo of Savoy, who abdicated in despair, and
a federal republic which had three presidents in a year and
finally broke up into factional anarchy, he supported the
restoration of the monarchy in the person of Isabel II's son
Alfonso XII, which took place at the end of 1874. Alarcón was
offered decorations and honours as well as high political posts
which he rejected on the grounds that he had originally supported the overthrow of Isabel in favour of her brother, the
Duke of Montpensier and nobody else. He did, however,
accept a seat in the Council of State.

Several of Alarcón's best-known works now appeared in
book form, although many of them had first appeared in
journals. In 1874 he published a travel diary, *La Alpujarra*,
about his native region, which included a picture of the last
rebellion of the forcibly converted Moorish inhabitants which
occurred in the sixteenth century. The same year, 1874, saw
the publication of the book for which he is best-known, *El
sombrero de tres picos* (*The Three-Cornered Hat*).

In 1875 and 1880 two novels, *El escándalo* and *El niño de la bola* appeared, of which the former seemed to show Alarcón as veering towards conservatism in his sympathetic portrayal of a Jesuit priest and in his views on the great religious debates of the time about the role of the Church in civil life. The latter novel however, contained certain aspects which threw doubt on the accusations that he had become a clerical obscurantist.

In 1876 Alarcón was elected almost unanimously to the *Real Academia Española*. *El Capitán Veneno* appeared in 1881 and his last novel, *La pródiga*, in the following year. Attacked by the critics who had generally shown themselves hostile to his more serious works of fiction, on the grounds that he had shown himself pro-clerical in his views on the role of the Church in the State, Alarcón spent the rest of his life in a country house at Valdemoro, south of Madrid, where he constructed a special pavilion for writing and edited his *Complete Works*.

He died in 1891, having suffered from partial paralysis for some time.

*

Alarcón had been asked to send a humorous story to a Cuban literary magazine to which he contributed. Remembering from his childhood, as he tells us in his preface, the folktale of the *Corregidor and the Miller's Wife*, he wrote a short-story version in less than twenty-four hours. He was about to post it when he recognized its potential and decided to rewrite it as a novel. It then first appeared in a Madrid magazine.

With *Don Quixote*, *The Three-Cornered Hat* shares the merit of being probably the best-known work of Spanish literature outside Spain. This has not been due only to Manuel de Falla's ballet suite based on the novel, for translations and editions for non-Spanish readers were published soon after its appearance. The story, strongly reminiscent in its intrigue of an eighteenth-century opera, stands or falls on its capacity to amuse. It has no profound message, except Alarcón's light-hearted attack on Absolutism, personified by the Corregidor who soon discovers that he is certainly not absolute as far as his wife is concerned. There is no deep study of character, though sufficient indications are given for the personages to live for the duration of the story. There are certainly elements of *costumbrismo*, in the deft pictures of Andalusian life around which the tale is constructed, but everything is subordinated to the clarity and speed of the plot.

Captain Poison is an underrated work, overshadowed by its famous companion, with which it is often printed. Without claiming any deep insights into human nature, it takes a highly probable situation based on historical circumstances, sets it in a house in a street in the centre of Madrid, uses characters who have considerable depth and little by little shows the changes in their attitudes and relationship. Its very ease demonstrates a high order of ability to select possibilities of plot-development and great skill in the writing of dialogue. Here again, Alarcón is seen as a superb craftsman.

The short stories also possess the Alarcón characteristic of deftness and their speed and verve succeed in masking the large amount of contrivance and coincidence which they use. But the demand on the reader willingly to surrender his disbelief becomes evident only on close examination and the stories stand by their pace, their vivid portrayals and descriptions and the realism of their circumstances.

MICHAEL ALPERT
January 1974

THE THREE-CORNERED HAT

A true story of an event commemorated in ballads,
written now just as it happened.

Author's preface

FEW Spaniards, even including the least knowledgeable and
educated, do not know the popular little story which is the
basis of this short work.

An ignorant goatherd, who had never left the isolated
hamlet where he was born, was the first person whom we
ever heard tell it. He was one of those rustics who are absolutely uneducated but naturally clever and funny, who so often
appear in our literature under the name of *pícaros*. Whenever
there was a fiesta in the hamlet, for a wedding or a baptism,
or when the landlord and his lady made a formal visit, he was
in charge of the funmaking and the mimicry, the clowning
and the ballads and stories in verse. And it was precisely on
one of those occasions (almost a whole life ago), that is to say,
over thirty-five years, that he saw fit to dazzle and enmesh our
innocence (relative) one night with the verse tale of the
Corregidor* and the Miller's Wife or *The Miller and the Corregidor's Wife*, that today we offer to the public under the more
transcendental and philosophical title (for the seriousness of
our times requires such) of *The Three-Cornered Hat*.

We also remember that, while the goatherd was so greatly
amusing us, the unmarried girls sitting around blushed deeply,
from which their mothers deduced that the story was a little
blue and so they reproved the goatherd. But poor Repela,
(that was the goatherd's name) didn't stop for that and said in
answer that there was no reason for them to be shocked, be-

* The King's representative responsible for the administration of
justice and for overseeing local government.

cause there was nothing in his tale that nuns and even little four-year-old girls did not know.

'And, if you don't agree, tell me,' asked the goatherd, 'what do we learn from the story of the *Corregidor and the Miller's Wife*? That married folk sleep together and that no married man likes another man to sleep with his wife! I don't think that's news!'

'True, true,' replied the mothers, hearing their daughters' peals of laughter.

'The proof that old Repela is right,' said the father of the bridegroom, 'is that all the children and adults here present already know that, as soon as the dancing is over tonight, Juan and Manolilla will sleep for the first time in that handsome double bed that old Gabriela has just shown our daughters for them to admire the embroidery on the pillow-cases.'

'That's not all,' said the bride's grandfather, 'even in the Holy Book and in the sermons themselves the children are told about all these really very natural things. They tell them about Saint Anne's long barrenness, the virtue of chaste Joseph in Egypt, Judith's trick and many other miracles which I can't recall at the moment. And so, ladies and gentlemen . . .'

'Don't take any notice, Repela,' exclaimed the girls boldly, 'tell us the tale again; it's very funny!'

'And very moral too,' went on the grandfather, 'because it doesn't tell anybody to be bad, nor does it tell them how to be so, nor is anybody who is bad allowed to get off scot-free . . .'

'Go on, tell it again,' said the mothers at last, having reached their decision.

Then old Repela told the ballad again. And when everybody had considered its text in the light of such ingenuous criticism, they found that there was no but to be butted, which means that they granted it the necessary *imprimatur potest*.

*

As the years have passed, we have heard many different versions of that same story of *The Miller and the Corregidor's Wife*, always told by village and farmyard humorists like the long-dead Repela. We have also seen it in print, in various blind man's Ballads* and even in the famous ballad collection of the unforgettable Don Agustín Durán.

The basis of the story is the same: tragi-comical, jocose and terribly witty, like all the dramatic moral lessons that our people love. But its form, the mechanism of the particular version, the individual twists, are very, very different from the goatherd's story, so much so that he would never have been able to recite any of these versions in that hamlet, not even the ones which are in print, unless the decent girls covered their ears beforehand or risked their mother's rage. To such an extent have the vulgar bumpkins of other parts of the country distorted and exaggerated the traditional legend that was so rich, funny and delicate in Repela's classic version!

And so, a long time ago we conceived the idea of re-establishing the truth, by giving this rare and wonderful story back its original character, where we never doubted that decorum came off best. How can it be doubted? When this sort of story gets into the hands of the common people, it never changes for the better, to become more lovely, delicate and moral; it just becomes spoilt and tarnished on contact with vulgarity and lewdness.

That is the story of this book . . . so let's plunge in . . . that is, let us begin the story of *The Corregidor and the Miller's Wife*, not without hoping from your healthy judgement, dear reader, that, 'after reading it and crossing yourself more times than if you had seen the Devil' as *Estebanillo Gómez* wrote when beginning his story, 'you will own that it is worthy and deserving of being brought to light'.

July 1874

* Compositions sung by blind beggars and sold by them in printed form.

CHAPTER I

When it Happened

THIS long century, which is already drawing to its close, was just beginning. The exact year is not known. It is only established that it was after 1804 and before 1808.

So Don Carlos IV of Bourbon was still reigning in Spain, 'By the Grace of God', according to his coins, and by the oblivion or especial grace of Bonaparte, according to the French *Gazettes*. The other European sovereigns who descended from Louis XIV had already lost their crowns (and the chief of them his head) in the violent storm which had swept this ancient part of the world since 1789.

The singularity of our country in those times was not limited to this. The Soldier of the Revolution, son of an obscure Corsican lawyer, victor of Rivoli, the Pyramids, Marengo and a hundred other battles, had just crowned himself with the crown of Charlemagne and changed Europe completely by creating and abolishing nations, erasing frontiers, inventing dynasties and changing the form, names, places, customs and even dress of the countries through which he passed on his warhorse like a living earthquake, or like the Antichrist, as the Northern Powers called him . . .

Our ancestors – God rest their souls – far from hating or fearing him, took pleasure in exaggerating his fantastic deeds, as if he were the hero of a book of chivalry, or of things happening on another planet. It never even occurred to them that he might come here to perpetrate the atrocities he had committed in France, Italy, Germany and other countries. Once a week – twice at the most – the post came from Madrid to most of the major towns in the peninsular, bringing an issue or two of the *Gazette* – which didn't come out daily either – and from it, assuming the *Gazette* mentioned the subject, the local dignitaries would discover whether there was now one more state or one less on the other side of the Pyrenees; if there had been another battle in which six or seven kings or emperors had fought; and whether Napoleon was to be found in Milan, Brussels or Warsaw. Outside this, our forbears lived in the old Spanish style, very slowly, clinging to their time-consecrated customs, in the peace and grace of God, with their Inquisition and their friars, their picturesque inequality before the law, their personal privileges, rights and exemptions, their lack of any local or political freedom, governed jointly by notable bishops and powerful *corregidors*, that is, magistrates appointed by the King (it was not easy to separate the respective powers of the two, because both had a finger in the temporal and eternal pie). Our ancestors paid tithes, first-fruits, sales taxes, Royal levy, obligatory contributions and offerings, taxes, minor taxes, poll tax, Royal tax, duties, income tax and maybe fifty more taxes whose nomenclature is not to the point now.

And this is all that our story has to do with the military and political history of that time, for the only purpose in telling what was happening in the world then was to show that, in the year in question – let us suppose it was 1805 – Spain was still ruled according to the *ancien régime* in all spheres of private and public life, as if, in the midst of so many new developments and upheavals, the Pyrenees had become another great wall of China.

CHAPTER 2

How People Lived at That Time

In Andalusia, for example, because what you are about to hear happened, as a matter of fact, in a city in Andalusia, people of distinction still rose very early, and went to early Mass in the cathedral even if it was not a day of obligation. At nine they breakfasted on a fried egg, a cup of chocolate and pieces of toast. Between one and two they lunched on stew and a meat course if there was any game and, if not, on stew by itself. After lunch they took a siesta and then went for a walk in the country. At dusk they went and recited the Rosary at their respective parish churches, with another cup of chocolate at the Angelus, this time with biscuits. The leaders of society attended the reception given by the *Corregidor* or the Dean or the titled person who resided in the town, and they all went home at the hour when the prayers for the dead are said, closing their doors before the curfew bell. For supper they ate salad and ragout, to give the stew another name, if no fresh anchovies had come. Then those who were married went to bed immediately with their wives, not without previously having warmed the bed in nine months out of the twelve.

A happy time it was when our land still remained in peaceful possession of all the spider's webs, dust, woodworm, respect, faith, traditions, uses and abuses sanctified by the centuries! A fortunate time, I repeat . . . particularly for poets who could find a one-act play, a sketch, a comedy, a drama, a religious play or an epic around every corner, instead of this prosaic uniformity and insipid realism that was the final legacy to us of the French Revolution! A fortunate time, yes indeed!

But all this is going over old ground. Let us have an end of generalities and plunge resolutely into the story of *The Three-Cornered Hat*.

CHAPTER 3

One Good Turn Deserves Another

AND SO, at that time, near the city of — there was a famous flour-mill, which no longer exists, situated about a quarter of a league from the town between the foot of a gentle hill covered with mazzard and cherry trees and a most fertile piece of cultivated land which acted as the border and sometimes the bed of the irregular, treacherous so-called river.

For many and various reasons, the mill had been for some time the favourite place which the best-known personages of the city made for in their walks and where they rested. In the first place, it was reached by a carter's path, less impassable than the others in the locality. In the second place, in front of the mill was a little stone-floored yard, covered with an enormous climbing vine, under which it was very pleasant to enjoy the cool in the summer and the sun in the winter, thanks to the alternative appearance and disappearance of the foliage. In the third place, the miller was a very respectful, discreet and elegant man, who, as is said, 'knew how to get on with people' and who gave the gentlemen who honoured him by attending his evening gathering, whatever was in season, either green beans, or cherries and mazzards, or unripened lettuces on the stalk, which are very good to eat with the macaroons made of bread dough and olive oil, which Their Lordships had ordered previously and sent on in advance. At other times there were melons, or grapes from that same vine which acted as a canopy, or toasted maize, if it was winter, and roast chestnuts and almonds and nuts and, sometimes, on very cold afternoons, a glass of home-made wine inside the house and in the friendly light of the lamp, to which at Christmas would be added some honeyed fritters, shortbread, crescent rolls or slices of ham from the Alpujarras mountains.

'Was the miller so rich, or his guests so tactless?' you will interrupt me to exclaim.

Neither the one nor the other. The Miller had only enough to live on and those gentlemen were delicacy and pride personified. But at a time when one paid fifty or so different taxes to the Church and the State, a rustic as intelligent as he was, risked little by earning the goodwill of aldermen, canons, friars, notaries and other people of position. And so there were plenty of people who said that Lucas, that was the Miller's name, saved a mint of money every year by treating everybody.

'I'd be very obliged if Your Worship would give me one of the little old doors from the house you knocked down,'

he would say to one.

'I'd be obliged if Your Worship could tell them to reduce my Royal levy or my sales tax or my income tax,'

he would say to another.

'Will Your Reverence let me cut some leaves for my silk-worms in the monastery garden?'

'I'd be obliged if Your Reverence would give me permission to collect some firewood from this or that heath.'

'Would Your Grace write a note so that I can cut a little wood in such and such a pine forest?'

'I need Your Honour to write me out a little document as a favour.'

'I can't pay the ground rent this year.'

'I hope they'll find for me in my case.'

'I hit so-and-so today and I hope he goes to prison for provoking me.'

'Would Your Worship have such-and-such to spare?'

'Can you lend me the mule?'

'Are you using the cart tomorrow?'

'Could I send for the donkey?' . . .

And this went on all the time and the answer was always a generous and unselfish one:

'Whatever you like . . .'

So you can see that Lucas was not on the way to being ruined.

CHAPTER 4

A Woman Seen from the Outside

THE last and perhaps the most powerful reason for the gentry of the city to frequent Lucas's mill in the afternoons was that clergymen and laymen, beginning with My Lord Bishop and His Honour the *Corregidor* could contemplate at their ease one of the most beautiful, charming and marvellous works that ever left the hand of God, called at the time the 'Supreme Being' by Jovellanos and all the school of imitators of the French that were in our country at the time.

This work was called . . . Señora Frasquita.

I shall begin to answer your questions by saying that Señora Frasquita, wife of Lucas in the eyes of God and Man, was a decent woman and all the illustrous visitors to the mill knew it. I'll go further: none of them ever showed signs of looking at her with a man's eye or with a sinful thought in the back of his mind. They certainly admired her and sometimes paid her compliments – in front of her husband, of course. They all did so, the friars and the gentlemen, the canons and the beruffed magistrates, for she was a marvel of beauty who did honour to her Creator and, like a female devil in maliciousness and coquetry, she innocently cheered up the most downcast spirits.

'She's a fine soul,' the most virtuous Prelate would say.

'She's a statue of Hellenic antiquity,' observed a very erudite lawyer, a corresponding member of the Academy of History.

'She's Eve herself come to life again,' burst out the Prior of the Franciscan monastery.

'She's a fine figure of a girl,' exclaimed the colonel.

'She's a serpent, a siren, a devil!' added the *Corregidor*. 'But she's a good woman, an angel, a babe, a little girl of four,' they all agreed as they returned from the mill stuffed with grapes or nuts, on the way to their gloomy and dull homes.

The little girl of four, that is, Señora Frasquita, was close on thirty; she was over five-and-a-half feet tall and solid in proportion, or perhaps even solider than her imposing height called for. She looked like a huge Niobe, even without her children. She was like a feminine Hercules. She seemed a Roman matron of the type that can still be seen in the Trastevere. But what attracted the attention most was her mobility, the speed, animation and grace of her imposing bulk. Before she could be a statue as the worthy Academician had called her, she would need to acquire the calm of a monument. She swayed like a reed, turned like a weathercock and danced like a top. Her face was even more mobile and thus less sculptured. It was enlivened charmingly by as many as five dimples; two in one cheek, one in the other, another, a very small one, next to the left hand side of her mouth where her laughing lips met, and the last and very large one, right in the middle of her round chin. Add to all this her cheeky grimaces, her amusing winks and all the different ways she held her head which made her conversation so pleasant, and you can form an idea of that face, which was so full of wit and beauty and always radiant with health and happiness.

Neither Señora Frasquita nor Lucas were Andalusians. She was Navarrese and he was from Murcia. He had come to the city of — at the age of fifteen, partly as a page and partly as a servant to the Bishop who had preceded the one who was now in charge of that see. His protector educated him for the cloth and it was perhaps with this in view and perhaps so that he should not be short of the proper sustenance to maintain him, that he bequeathed him the mill. But Lucas had only taken Minor Orders when His Grace died, so there and then he hung up his habit and joined the Army, more eager as he was to see the world and find adventure than to say Mass or mill wheat. In 1793 he fought in the campaign in the western Pyrenees, as orderly to the valiant General Don Ventura Caro. He was present when the Castle of Piñón was stormed and then remained for a long time in the northern provinces, where he was finally discharged. In Estella he met Señora Frasquita, who was then known only as Frasquita. He won her love, married her and took her away to Andalusia to search the mill which would watch them living so peacefully and happily during the rest of their pilgrimage through this vale of tears and laughter.

But, though Señora Frasquita had been brought from Navarre to that lonely place, she had acquired no Andalusian habits and was very different from the local countrywomen. She dressed in a more simple, casual and elegant style than they, washed her person more and allowed the sun and the wind to caress her arms below her rolled-up sleeves and her open neck. To a certain degree she dressed in the style of the ladies of the epoch, the style of the ladies of Goya, the dress of Queen Maria Luisa: if not a skirt allowing her to take half a step, one which permitted her one step at the most, very short, revealing her tiny feet and the beginning of the curve of her magnificent legs. She wore round, low necklines, in the Madrid style, for she had stopped for two months in that city with her Lucas on the way from Navarre to Andalusia. She wore all her hair gathered up on top, which allowed full play to the grace of her head and the elegance of her neck. She wore an earring in each tiny ear and many rings on the slender fingers of her hard but clean hands. Finally, Señora Frasquita's voice carried all the tones of the most expressive and melodious instrument and her laughter was so happy and silvery that it was like a peal of bells on Easter Saturday.

Now let us draw a portrait of Lucas.

CHAPTER 5

A Man from Outside and from Within

LUCAS was uglier than sin. He had been so all his life and he was now close on forty years old. Nevertheless few more agreeable and charming men had been brought into the world by God. Taken by his liveliness, his wit and his charm, the late Bishop had asked his parents to entrust him to his care. They were shepherds, but of sheep, not of souls.

When His Grace died, and the lad had left the seminary for the barracks, General Caro honoured him among all the Army and made him his most personal orderly, his real field batman. When at last his military obligations were over, Lucas found it as easy to win the heart of Señora Frasquita as it had been to gain the affection of the Bishop and the General. The Navarrese girl, who was twenty at the time and the darling of all the young men of Navarre, some of them quite rich, could not resist the never-ending shafts of wit, the amusing comments, the eyes of a lovesick monkey, and the innocent and ever-present smile, full of malice but also of gentleness, of the Murcian who was so daring, so loquacious, so sharp, so ready, so valiant and so amusing that in the end he turned the head not only of the beautiful girl he desired, but also of her father and mother.

At that time, and still at the time of which we are writing, Lucas was a man of rather small stature (at least in comparison with his wife), rather bulky in the shoulders, very dark, smooth-chinned, with a long nose, big ears and pitted with smallpox. On the other hand, his mouth was well-proportioned and his teeth were excellent. One might say that only the outside of the man was crude and ugly. As soon as you began to see inside him, his good qualities became evident, and these began with his teeth. Then came his voice. It was vibrant, varied in tone and attractive. Sometimes it was manly and deep, gentle and honeyed when he wanted something and always difficult to resist. Then came what that voice said: everything was pertinent, witty, amusing and persuasive. And finally, Lucas's character was brave, loyal and honourable. He was a man of commonsense, he wanted to learn and yet he knew many things, instinctively and empirically. He scorned the foolish profoundly whatever their social class. Then he had a certain spirit of irony, mockery and sarcasm which, in the eyes of the Academician, made him seem an unpolished version of our great satirist, Don Francisco de Quevedo.

Such was Lucas, from the outside and from the inside.

CHAPTER 6

Skills of the Couple

So Señora Frasquita was deeply in love with Lucas and thought herself the luckiest woman in the world because he adored her also. They had no children, as we already know, and thus had dedicated themselves to attending to and spoiling each other with indescribable care, but without their tender solicitude becoming sentimental and cloying because it was so affected, as so often happens in childless couples. Quite the contrary; they treated each other with frankness, happiness, humour and trust, like children who play with each other and adore each other with all their hearts without ever saying so or even realizing the nature of their feelings.

There could never have been a better-combed, better-dressed miller, or a man more pampered in his food or more surrounded with comforts in his home, than Lucas! No miller's wife and no queen could have been surrounded by so much care, flattery and delicacy than was Señora Frasquita! And no mill could include within its walls so many necessary, useful, agreeable, amusing and even unnecessary things as the one which is about to be the scene of almost the whole of this story!

The greater part of the credit for this went to Señora Frasquita, the neat, hardworking, strong and healthy girl from Navarre, who knew how, was willing, and was able to cook, sew, embroider, sweep, make pastries, wash, iron, whitewash the house, polish the copper, knead, weave, knit, sing, dance, play the guitar and the castanets, play cribbage and bezique and a host of other things which it would be endless to relate. And the credit went no less to Lucas, who knew how to, was willing and able to run the mill, cultivate the land, hunt, fish, work as a carpenter, a blacksmith and a mason, and help his wife in all the chores of the house, read, write, cast accounts, etc.

And this is not to mention his specialities, that is his exceptional abilities.

For example, Lucas loved flowers (just like his wife) and was such a skilled gardener, that he had managed to produce new strains by means of patient grafting. He had some natural skill as an engineer and had demonstrated it by building a dam, a siphon and an aqueduct which tripled the water available for the mill. He had taught a dog to dance, tamed a snake and trained a parrot to sing out the hours according to a sun clock which he had drawn on a wall. The result was that the parrot proclaimed the time most exactly, even on cloudy days and during the night.

Finally, the mill had a vegetable garden which grew all sorts of fruit and vegetables, a pond enclosed by a circle of jasmines where Lucas and Señora Frasquita bathed in the summer, a garden, a hothouse or conservatory for exotic plants, a spring of drinking-water, two donkeys on which the couple went to town or to the neighbouring villages, a chicken run, dovecote, aviary, fishpond hatchery, silkworm nursery, beehives, whose bees sucked the jasmines, wine press and wine cellar, both on a very small scale, oven, loom, forge, carpenter's workshop etc. All of this was contained in an eight-roomed house with two *fanegas* (three acres) of land, and with a taxable value of ten thousand *reales*.

CHAPTER 7

The Bases of Happiness

CERTAINLY, the miller and his wife loved each other and it might even have been thought that she loved him more than he loved her, in spite of his being so ugly and she so beautiful. I mention this because Señora Frasquita used to be jealous and questioned Lucas when he was late coming back from town or from the villages where he went for grain. On the other hand, Lucas was even rather pleased to see the attention paid to Señora Frasquita by the gentlemen who frequented the mill. He was proud and rejoiced that she pleased them all as much as she did him and, although in his heart he knew that some of them envied him and desired her like simple mortals and would have given anything for her to be a less respectable woman, he still left her alone for days on end without the least care and he never asked her later what she had done or who had been there while he had been away.

All the same, this was not to say that Lucas's love was less deep than Señora Frasquita's. It meant that he trusted her virtue more than she did his. He was more far-seeing than she and he knew how much he was loved and how greatly his wife respected herself. Basically, Lucas was a real man, a man like the Shakespearian character, with a few unshakable feelings, incapable of doubts, who believed or died, loved or killed, and understood no shades of meaning or levels between supreme contentment or the death of his happiness.

In other words, he was a Murcian Othello, wearing rope-soled slippers and a cloth hat, in the first act of a possible tragedy.

But, why these tragic notes in such a happy tune? Why these fateful shafts of lightning in such a calm atmosphere? Why those melodramatic postures in such a traditional scene?

You are about to be told the reason.

CHAPTER 8

The Man in the Three-Cornered Hat

IT was two o'clock one October afternoon. The cathedral bell was tolling Vespers, which meant that all the important people in the town had already had lunch. The canons were making their way to the choir and the laymen to their bed-rooms to sleep the siesta, especially those who by reason of their professions, that is the municipal Fathers, had spent the entire morning at work.

So it was very odd that at such a time, most unsuitable for walking because of the heat, the illustrious Señor *Corregidor* of the town should walk out of it with only one constable to attend him. Clearly it was the *Corregidor*, for nobody could mistake him, by day or by night, because of the immense size of his three-cornered hat, the brilliance of his crimson cloak and his peculiarly grotesque mien.

There are still many people with clear recollections of the three-cornered hat and the crimson cloak. I am one, just as everyone of us born in that town in the latter years of the

28

reign of Fernando VII can remember seeing them hanging from a nail, the only adornment on a tumbledown wall in the crumbling tower of the house His Lordship occupied, a tower used as a playground by his grandchildren in latter years. The two old-fashioned garments, that cape and that hat – the black hat on top and the red cape below – forming a ghost of Absolutism, a sort of preserved winding-sheet, a kind of retrospective caricature of his power, painted in soot and red ochre like so many other cartoons that we young *Constitutionalists* of 1837 who met there used to daub; in short, like a scarecrow who in earlier times had been a scareman. Today I shiver at the thought that I ridiculed him by parading his clothes around the town at carnival time, mounted on a chimney brush, and that they were used as a comic disguise by the idiot who raised the biggest laugh from the crowd . . . poor *Principle of Authority*! How those of us who invoke you so often now treated you then!

As for the grotesque mien of the Señor *Corregidor*, it consisted, they say, in that his shoulders were . . . heavy, even more than Lucas's . . . almost hunchbacked, to call a spade a spade; he was under medium height, skinny, sickly, bow-legged and walked in a style very much his own, swaying from side to side and from back to front. The only way to describe his gait is to say, though it sounds absurd, that he looked lame in both legs. On the other hand, tradition adds, his features were quite regular but already quite wrinkled because of his complete lack of teeth. His complexion was olive green, like most Castilians, with large dark eyes, in which anger, tyranny and sensuality shone together; his features were thin and wicked, and revealed, not personal courage, but crafty malice capable of anything and a certain air of self-satisfaction partly aristocratic and partly libertine, which betrayed that in his remote youth the man had been pleasing and successful with women, in spite of his bow legs and hump.

Don Eugenio de Zúñiga y Ponce de León (that was His Lordship's name) had been born in Madrid of a noble family; at the time of this story he was about fifty-five years old and for four years had been the *corregidor* of the town, where soon after his arrival he married the noble lady we shall mention later.

Don Eugenio's stockings (the only thing besides his shoes that could be seen under his enormous crimson cloak), were white and he wore black shoes with gilt buckles. But when the heat of the open countryside obliged him to open his cloak, he was seen to be wearing a batiste neckcloth, a serge waist-coat of a light-blue colour, heavily embroidered in green, short breeches of black silk and an enormous coat of the same material as the waistcoat, a short dress sword with a steel guard, a stick with tassels and a fine pair of gloves of straw-coloured chamois that he never put on but merely held like a sceptre.

The constable who walked twenty-five paces behind the *Corregidor* was called Garduña or Weasel, and the name was well chosen. Skinny, lithe, his eyes darting in front and behind, to the left and right of him as he walked along, he had a long neck, a tiny, repugnant face and hands like two bundles of birch rods. He looked at one and the same time exactly like a ferret to track criminals, the rope to bind them and the instrument to punish them.

The first *corregidor* who set eyes on him had said there and then:

'You shall be my real constable.'

And he had already served four *corregidors*.

He was forty-eight years old and wore a three-cornered hat, much smaller than his master's (the latter's, you will remember, was quite extraordinarily large), his cloak was black as were his stockings and his entire suit. He carried a stick with-out tassels and a sort of roasting-spit for a sword.

That black scarecrow was like the shadow of his gaudy master.

CHAPTER 9

'Giddy Up, Donkey!'

WHENEVER that worthy and his appendage passed, the labourers looked up from their toil and swept the ground with their hats in salutation, with more fear than respect, followed by a muttered:

'The Señor *Corregidor*'s off early to see Señora Frasquita this afternoon.'

'Early . . . and alone,' added some, who were accustomed to seeing him go that way in the company of several other people.

''Ere, Manuel, why d'ye think the Señor *Corregidor*'s off by himself to see her today?' said a village woman to her husband, from her place side-saddle behind him on their mule.

And as she asked him the question she tickled him to make her point.

'Stop thinking the worst of people, Josefa,' exclaimed the man, 'Señora Frasquita just couldn't . . .'

'I'm not saying she could. But that doesn't mean the *Corregidor* doesn't fancy her. Of all that lot who go to those parties up at the mill I've heard he's the only one who's got nasty ideas. There's another of these Madrid fellows for you, always after the girls.'

'How do you know whether he's after the girls or not?' asked the husband in his turn.

'I'm not saying so from personal experience. He may be the *Corregidor*, but he'd be careful about starting with me!'

The woman was ugly, extremely ugly.

'Well, so what? Good luck to them!' retorted Manuel. 'I don't reckon Lucas would let her . . . bad temper he's got if you get on the wrong side of him.'

'Yes, but it wouldn't do him any harm.' Josefa grimaced meaningly.

'Lucas is a respectable man,' answered her husband, 'and some things just can't be done . . .'

'Well, there you are, let them get on with it. If I was Señora Frasquita . . .!'

'Giddy up, donkey!' shouted her husband to change the subject, and the donkey began to trot, so the rest of the dialogue was lost to hearing.

CHAPTER 10

From the Climbing Vine

AT the time the labourers were greeting the *Corregidor* and making their comments, Señora Frasquita was carefully watering and sweeping the stone-paved yard which served as an entrance or courtyard to the mill, and placing half a dozen chairs under the thickest part of the vine, into which Lucas had climbed to cut the best bunches of grapes which he was now arranging artistically in a basket.

'Well, yes, Frasquita,' said Lucas from his perch high up in the vine, 'the Señor *Corregidor* is in love with you, and in a very nasty way!'

'I told you that a long time ago,' she answered, 'but let him suffer! Careful, Lucas, careful you don't fall!'

'Don't worry, I'm holding on tight, and you've obviously taken the fancy of the . . .'

'Look, I don't want any more news!' she interrupted. 'I know only too well who fancies me and who doesn't. I only wish I knew as well why you don't!'

'Because you're very ugly! See?' answered Lucas.

'Now, look here, ugly and all, I can get up that vine and knock you off your perch head first!'

'More likely I wouldn't let you get down and I'd eat you up!'

'Oh yes? And when all my suitors came and saw us there, we'd look like a monkey and his mate!'

'They'd be right too, because you're a gorgeous little monkey-face and with my hump I look just like an ape.'

'I love your hump . . .!'

'Then you'll like the *Corregidor*'s even more, because it's bigger than mine.'

'Now, now, Señor Don Lucas! You shouldn't be jealous'.

'Me? Jealous of that old humbug? Quite the opposite, I'm rather happy that he's in love with you.'

'Why?'

'Because sin brings its own punishment. You will never really love him and meanwhile I'm the real *Corregidor* of the city.'

'Look at the show-off! Imagine what would happen if I did fall in love with him. Stranger things than that have happened!'

'It wouldn't worry me either.'

'Why?'

'Because you wouldn't be you any longer. And, if you weren't you, or as I think you are, what the hell would I care even if the devil carried you off?'

'Yes, but, what would you do if it did happen?'

'Me? I haven't the slightest idea because I'd be somebody else and not who I am now, so I can't imagine what I'd think . . .'

'But why would you be somebody else?' Frasquita persisted bravely, stopping her sweeping, and standing, arms akimbo, looking upwards.

Lucas scratched his head as if he were digging around to try and find a very important idea in it, and then at last, more anxiously and seriously than usual, he said:

'I'd be another man, because today I am a man who believes in you as he does in himself, and who only lives for this belief. So, if I stopped believing in you, I should die or change into another man. I should live in a different way. It would be like having just been born. My deepest feelings would be different. So I don't know how I should act towards you. I might laugh or I might turn my back on you . . . I might not even know you, I might . . . oh, but how we love getting into a bad mood without cause! What on earth does it matter if all the *corregidors* in the world are in love with you? Aren't you my Frasquita?'

33

'Yes, you fool,' she answered, unable to control her laughter. 'I'm your Frasquita, and you're my own darling Lucas, uglier than a bogeyman, cleverer than any other man, the best of all people and I love you more . . . when you come down from the vine I'll show you what I mean by love! You'd better get ready. I'm going to give you more slaps and pinches than you've hairs on your head! Quiet now! What's that I see? The Señor *Corregidor*'s coming this way quite alone. And so early too! He's got something in mind. It looks as if you were right!'

'Now, patience, and don't tell him I'm up here in the vine. He's coming to tell you in private how much he loves you. He thinks he's caught me having my siesta. I think I'll have a fine time hearing him explaining why he's come!'

And, as he said this, Lucas handed the basket down to his wife.

'That's not a bad idea!' she said, laughing again. 'Thinks he's clever, coming from Madrid? Thinks he's the *corregidor* for me as well, does he? But here he comes. Mind you, Garduña was a little way behind him and he's sat down in the ravine in the shade . . . what a pest! Now hide carefully between the branches and we'll have a bigger laugh than you think!'

And, saying this, the beautiful Navarrese woman began to sing a fandango, which she knew as well as the songs of her native land.

CHAPTER 11

The Bombardment of Pamplona

'GOOD afternoon, Frasquita!' whispered the *Corregidor*, emerging from under the vine-covered doorway and tiptoeing towards her.

'Good afternoon to you, sir,' she replied in a natural voice and with a curtsey. 'Fancy seeing Your Honour here at this time of day and in the heat too. Now, sit down, Your Honour, it's nice and cool here. Why didn't Your Honour wait for the other gentlemen? Their chairs are ready for them. This afternoon I'm expecting My Lord Bishop in person as he's promised my Lucas to come and give his opinion on our first grapes. And how's Your Lordship keeping? How's My Lady?'

The *Corregidor* was ill-at-ease. He had longed to be alone with Señora Frasquita and, now that he was, he felt a sense of unreality, or perhaps hostile Fate was playing a trick to make his success taste like ashes. So he contented himself with answering:

'It's not as early as you think. It must be about half past three.'

'It's quarter past two,' said Frasquita, looking squarely at him.

He said nothing, like a criminal unable to answer his accusers.

'What about Lucas? Is he asleep?' he asked, after a pause. It should be noted that like everybody who has lost all his teeth, the *Corregidor* spoke gummily and with a whistle, as if he were eating his own lips.

'Of course,' answered Frasquita, 'as soon as the clock strikes two he falls asleep wherever he is, even on the edge of a cliff.'

'Well then, let him sleep!' exclaimed the old man, growing even paler than he already was. 'And Frasquita, dear Frasquita, listen, listen, come here. Sit down here, next to me. I've so many things I want to say to you.'

'I'm sitting down already,' said the miller's wife, fetching a low chair and putting it down in front of the *Corregidor*, a few feet from him.

Once seated, Frasquita crossed one leg over the other, leaned forward, rested one elbow on her knee and her young, appealing face in her hand, and with her head slightly tilted, a smile on her lips, all her five dimples in evidence and her calm eyes fixed on the *Corregidor*, she awaited His Lordship's declarations like Pamplona awaiting bombardment, as so often happened in the Peninsular War.

The poor man made as if to speak and then sat there with

his mouth open, as if transfixed before such beauty, such wealth of attraction, such a magnificent woman with her alabaster skin, her ample form, her pure and smiling mouth and her deep blue eyes, created, one would think, by the brush of Rubens.

'Frasquita!' uttered the King's delegate faintly after a long pause, while his crabby little face, covered in sweat, standing out over his hump, expressed his immense yearning. 'Frasquita!'

'That's my name,' answered the girl from the Pyrenees, 'so?'

'Whatever you want,' went on the old man in a tone of ineffable tenderness.

'Well, what I want . . .' said the miller's wife, 'Your Honour already knows. I want Your Honour to appoint a nephew of mine who lives in Estella as Secretary to the Town Council here. In that way he can get away from those mountains where he's having a lot of difficulty.'

'I've told you, Frasquita, that's impossible. The present Secretary . . .'

'Is a thief, a drunkard and an idiot!'

'Yes, I know . . . but he's well in with the Life Aldermen and I can't appoint another without the agreement of the Council. Otherwise, I run the risk . . .'

'Run the risk, run the risk! You know that even the cats in this house would run a risk for Your Lordship!'

'If I paid the price, would you love me?' stammered the *Corregidor*.

'No, Sir, I love Your Honour for nothing.'

'Oh, please, don't be so formal! Just call me "you" or whatever you like! So, you will love me, yes? Tell me.'

'Haven't I told you that I love you already?'

'But . . .'

'But nothing. You'll see what a fine-looking and decent chap my nephew is.'

'You're a fine-looker, Frasquita.'

'You like me?'

'Do I like you? There isn't a woman like you.'

'Well look, there's nothing false here,' answered Señora Frasquita, as she finished rolling up the sleeve of her dress and showed the *Corregidor* the rest of her arm, worthy of a caryatid and whiter than a lily.

'Do I like you?' went on the *Corregidor*. 'By day, at night, at all times, everywhere, I think of you!'

'Well then! Don't you like Her Ladyship?' asked Frasquita with such badly feigned compassion in her voice that it would have made even a hypochondriac laugh. 'What a pity! My Lucas told me that he had the pleasure of seeing her and talking to her when he went to repair your bedroom clock, and he said she's very pretty, very good, and has a kind nature.'

'Not all that kind, not all that marvellous,' muttered the *Corregidor* somewhat bitterly.

'On the other hand, other people have told me,' went on the miller's wife, 'that she's very bad-tempered, and very jealous and that you fear her more than a green switch!'

'No, it's not quite like that, my dear,' repeated Don Eugenio de Zúñiga y Ponce de León, growing red. 'You're exaggerating! My wife can be a little difficult, true enough, but there's a lot of difference between that and making me shake in my shoes. I am the *Corregidor*!'

'But, once and for all, do you love her or don't you?'

'I'll tell you. I love her very much, or rather I loved her before I met you. But I don't know what's got into me since I saw you and she herself knows that something's up. I tell you that if I hold my wife's face, now, it's as if I were holding my own. You see that I can't love her more than I do nor have any less feeling for her! But I'd give anything, including what I don't have, to be able to take hold of your hand, your arm, your face, your waist!'

And as he spoke, the *Corregidor* tried to seize the bare arm that Señora Frasquita was almost rubbing across his eyes. But, without losing her calm, she stretched out her hand and touched His Lordship's chest with the gentle violence and irresistible force of an elephant's trunk, and pushed him over on his back, chair and all.

'*Ave Maria Purisima*,' exclaimed the girl, almost doubled up with laughter. 'It looks as if the chair was broken.'

'What's going on down there?' exclaimed Lucas just then, his ugly face peeping from between the branches of the climbing vine.

The *Corregidor* was still flat on his back on the ground staring with indescribable terror at that man who appeared looking down on him from the sky.

It was as if His Lordship were the Devil, overcome not by Saint Michael, but by some other devil in hell.

'What d'you think is happening?' Señora Frasquita hastily replied. 'The Señor *Corregidor* didn't make sure the chair was steady, he began to rock, and then fell over!'

'*Jesús, María y José*!' exclaimed the miller in his turn. 'And has Your Lordship hurt himself? Would you like a little vinegar and water?'

'I'm quite all right,' said the *Corregidor*, getting up as best he could.

And then he added under his breath, but so that Frasquita could hear, 'You'll pay for this, both of you.'

'On the other hand, Your Lordship has saved my life,' answered Lucas without moving from his perch high up in the vine. 'Can you believe it, my dear, I was sitting up here looking at the grapes when I dropped off to sleep on these interlacing vine branches and twigs which leave just enough room for my body to fall through. So if Your Lordship's fall hadn't woken me just in time, this afternoon I should have broken my head on those stones.'

'Oh yes? Really? Yes,' answered the *Corregidor*. 'Well, my good man, I'm very happy . . . I mean I'm very happy I fell down!'

'You'll pay for this,' he added at once, to the miller's wife!

And he uttered these words in such a tone of concentrated rage that Señora Frasquita's face fell.

She understood clearly that the *Corregidor* had been startled at first, thinking that the miller had heard everything, but, once he was sure he had not heard anything (for Lucas's calm poker face would have deceived the sharpest observer) he began to indulge in all his anger and to conceive plans for revenge.

'Now then! Down you come and help me to brush His Lordship; he's got his clothes covered in dust,' exclaimed the miller's wife.

And, while Lucas climbed down, she said to the *Corregidor*, slapping her apron over his waistcoat and a few times round his ears:

'The poor fellow didn't hear anything. He was sleeping like a log.'

Not only these words, but much more the fact that she said them in a low voice as if the two were accomplices in a secret deed, produced a marvellous effect.

'You little devil! You wanton!' stuttered Don Eugenio de Zúñiga, suddenly overcome with tenderness, but still grumbling.

'Is Your Honour still angry with me?' wheedled the Navarrese girl.

The *Corregidor* saw that severity produced good results, so he tried to look at Señora Frasquita with an angry expression on his face. But he met her fascinating laugh and her divine eyes, in which shone the caress of a supplication. At once he went all soft and with a dribble and a whistle, where his total lack of teeth became more than ever evident, he said:

'It depends on you, my love.'

At that moment, Lucas swung down from the vine.

CHAPTER 12

Tithes and First-Fruits

THE *Corregidor* was re-established in his chair and the miller's wife glanced swiftly at her husband. She saw that not only was he as relaxed as always, but he was hard put to suppress the laughter that the recent occurrences had provoked in him. They threw each other a kiss, as soon as Don Eugenio looked away and then, with a voice so seductive that Cleopatra herself would have envied it, she said to him,

'Now Your Lordship must sample my grapes!'

That was a sight. If I had Titian's touch I should paint the beautiful Navarrese woman, just as she was then, standing in front of the mesmerized *Corregidor*, insolent, magnificent and provocative, with her proud figure, her tight dress, tall, her bare arms raised above her head, and a transparent bunch of grapes in each hand, as she said to him with an irresistible smile and a pleading and half-timid look:

'His Grace the Bishop hasn't tasted them yet . . . they're the first I've cut this year . . .'

She looked like some mighty Pomona offering fruits to a rural god, perhaps a satyr.

At that moment, at the other end of the paved yard the venerable Bishop of the diocese appeared, accompanied by the Lawyer-Academician and two canons of advanced age, and followed by his Secretary, two servants and two pages.

His Grace paused for a moment to contemplate that scene, so comic and so beautiful at the same time. At last, he said, in the reposed tone characteristic of the prelates of those days:

'The Fifth . . . pay tithes and first fruits to the Church of God, we are taught by Christian doctrine. But, Señor *Corregidor*, you are not content with administering the tithes, but you also try to eat the first fruits.'

'His Grace the Bishop,' exclaimed the miller and his wife as they left the *Corregidor* and ran to kiss the prelate's ring.

'God bless Your Grace, for coming to honour our humble dwelling!' said Lucas, with sincere veneration in his voice as he kissed the ring first.

'What a marvellously fine-looking Bishop I have!' exclaimed Señora Frasquita, as she bent to kiss the ring. 'God bless you and keep you longer for me than he kept Lucas's kind Bishop for him!'

'I don't know what good I can do you when you bless me instead of asking me for my blessing!' answered the kindly shepherd of souls with a laugh.

And, stretching out two fingers, he blessed Señora Frasquita and then the others standing round him.

'Here are the first fruits, Your Reverence and Grace,' said the *Corregidor* as he took a bunch from the hands of the miller's wife and presented it politely to the Bishop, 'I hadn't yet tasted the grapes.'

And, as the *Corregidor* uttered these words, he cast a swift and cynical glance at the splendid beauty of the miller's wife.

'Well, I'm sure that's not because they're green, like the ones in the fable,' commented the Academician.

'The ones in the fable, Señor Licentiate, were not green, but out of the fox's reach,' replied the Bishop.

Neither one nor the other had meant perhaps to allude to the *Corregidor*. But by chance both sentences were so apposite to what had just happened there that Don Eugenio de Zúñiga went livid with rage and said, as he kissed the prelate's ring,

'That is calling me a fox, Your Grace.'

'*Tu dixisti*,' the latter replied, with the benign severity of a saint, as, in fact, people say he was. '*Excusatio non petita, accusatio manifesta. Qualis vir, talis oratio.* But *satis jam dictum, nullus ultra sic sermo*, or, in other words, enough Latin and let's see these famous grapes.'

And he plucked just one grape from the bunch with which the *Corregidor* presented him.

'They're very good!' he exclaimed, looking at the grape against the light and handing it to his Secretary at once. 'What a pity they don't agree with me.'

The Secretary also looked at the grape, indicated polite admiration and handed it to one of the attendant clergy. The latter repeated the action of the Bishop and the gesture of the Secretary, going as far as to smell the grape and then put it in the basket with exquisite care, not without observing in a low voice to the party,

'His Grace is fasting . . .'

Lucas had been following the grape around. Now he craftily picked it up and ate it quickly without anyone seeing him.

After which, they all sat down. They talked about the

autumn, which was still very dry, in spite of the equinox with its usual storms having passed. They discussed the probability of another war between Napoleon and Austria. They insisted that Imperial troops would never invade Spanish territory. The lawyer complained of the times, so confused and calamitous, envying the tranquil epoch of his parents (as his parents had envied their grandparents' days). The parrot squawked five o'clock, and at a signal from the Reverend Bishop, the smaller of the pages went to the episcopal coach (which had been left in the same sandy ravine as Garduña, the constable), and returned with a magnificent cake of bread and oil, sprinkled with salt, which had left the oven scarcely an hour previously. A table was placed in the midst of the company. The cake was divided. Lucas and Frasquita, though they tried to refuse, were given their pieces ... and truly democratic equality reigned for half an hour under those vine tendrils through which filtered the last rays of the setting sun.

CHAPTER 13

Said the Kettle to the Pot

AN hour and a half later all the distinguished participants at the afternoon's buffet were back in town.

His Grace the Bishop and his company had arrived back quite early, thanks to their carriage, and were already in the palace where we shall leave them at their devotions.

The celebrated lawyer, who was very lean, and the two canons, who vied with each other in plumpness and presence, went with the *Corregidor* as far as the door of the Town Hall, where His Lordship said he had some work to do. Then they wended their way towards their respective homes, guiding themselves by the stars like sailors, or picking their way around corners like blind people, for night had already fallen. The moon had not yet appeared and public lighting (just like all the other enlightenment of this century) was still in the divine mind.

In contrast, it was not rare to see, flickering through the streets, some torch or lantern or other with which a humble servant guided his noble masters, who were going to their usual evening gathering or visiting a relative.

By almost every low barred window could be seen (or rather, could be sensed) a silent black mass. These were young men who, hearing steps, had ceased courting their girls for a moment.

'We're tearaways!' said the lawyer and the two canons to themselves as they hurried along. 'What will they think when they see us coming home at this time of night?'

'And what about people who meet us in the street like this, just after seven o'clock at night, like bandits under cover of darkness?'

'We've got to behave better than this.'

'Yes, yes. But that damned mill . . .'

'My wife said she's just about fed up with it,' said the Academician, in a tone which revealed his great fear of the next conjugal squabble.

'And what about my niece?' exclaimed one of the canons, who incidentally acted as the confessor. 'My niece says that priests shouldn't visit gossips!'

'All the same,' interrupted his companion, who was the official preacher, 'what we do there couldn't be more innocent.'

'I should say not! After all, even His Grace the Bishop goes there!'

'And then, gentlemen, at our age!' the confessor resumed. 'I was seventy-five yesterday.'

'Of course,' answered the other. 'But let's talk of something else. Wasn't Señora Frasquita beautiful this afternoon!'

'Oh, that . . . pretty, yes, you could say she's pretty,' said the lawyer, pretending to have no opinion in the matter.

'Very pretty,' said the confessor from inside his cloak.

'And, if you don't think so,' added the official preacher, 'ask the *Corregidor*.'

'The poor man's in love with her.'

'I should say he is!' exclaimed the cathedral confessor.

'Of course,' replied the corresponding Academician.

'Well, gentlemen, I have to go this way to get home earlier. A very good night to you!'

'Good night,' answered the two members of the cathedral Chapter.

And they walked on a few steps in silence.

'He also likes the miller's wife,' murmured the preacher, digging the confessor with his elbow.

'He makes it so obvious,' answered the latter, stopping at the door of his house, 'and what a clumsy fool he is! So, I'll see you tomorrow, my friend, I hope the grapes agree with you.'

'See you tomorrow, God willing. A very good night to you!'

'God give us a good night,' prayed the confessor, from his porch, which had a lantern and an image of the Virgin as well. And he rapped on the door with the knocker.

Once by himself in the street, the other canon, who was broader than he was tall, so much so that he looked as if he was rolling when he walked, proceeded home slowly. But before he got there, he stood against a wall and committed a certain offence which in later years would be the subject of a police notice. At the same time he said, doubtless thinking of his fellow canon:

'And you like Señora Frasquita as well. And the truth is,' he added after a moment, 'that, as pretty women go, she really is pretty!'

CHAPTER 14

The Advice of Garduña

MEANWHILE the *Corregidor* had gone up to the Town Hall, accompanied by Garduña, with whom he conversed, in the Council Hall, in a more familiar tone than normally corresponded to people of his class and office.

'Your Honour, mark the words of a beagle who knows

what hunting's about,' said the contemptible constable, 'Señora Frasquita is madly in love with you and everything Your Honour's just told me only helps to make me see that it's clearer than that light.'

And he pointed to an oil lamp, the type they make in Lucena, which scarcely illuminated an eighth of the hall.

'I'm not as sure as you, Garduña,' replied Don Eugenio, with a tired sigh.

'Well I don't know why not! But if that's so, let's speak frankly. Your Honour, and I beg your pardon, has something wrong with your body, isn't that so?'

'Well, yes,' replied the *Corregidor*. 'But Lucas has the same thing. He's got a bigger hump than me!'

'Much bigger! Very much bigger! Can't be compared in the slightest; but on the other hand – and this is what I was coming to – Your Honour's face is of very fine appearance . . . a handsome face, one might say, but Lucas is like Sergeant Utrera in the story, who was so ugly that he burst!'

The *Corregidor* smiled with some conceit.

'And another thing,' went on the constable, 'Señora Frasquita would jump off a cliff if that was the way to make sure her nephew got the job . . .'

'Now, there I agree with you. That job is my only hope!'

'Well then, shoulders to the wheel, Señor! I've explained my plan to Your Honour. All you've got to do is to put it into execution this very night!'

'I've told you lots of times that I don't need advice!' shouted Don Eugenio, remembering suddenly that he was speaking to his subordinate.

'I thought Your Honour had asked me . . .' stammered Garduña.

'Don't answer back!'

Garduña bowed.

'So, you were saying,' went on Señor de Zúñiga, cooling down a little, 'that it can all be settled tonight? Well now, my man, that's very good. By God it is! That way I'll not have to suffer this uncertainty for long.'

Garduña remained silent.

The *Corregidor* went to the table and wrote a few words on a sheet of official stamped paper, which he sealed and put away in the pocket of his coat-tail.

'That's the appointment for the nephew done!' he then said, taking a pinch of snuff. 'I'll settle it with the councillors tomorrow. Either they ratify it and agree or there'll be the biggest row you ever heard. Don't you think that's the way to do it?'

'That's it! That's it!' cried Garduña enthusiastically, putting his paw into the *Corregidor*'s box and taking a pinch of snuff. 'That's it! That's it! Your Honour's predecessor didn't bother about procedures either. Once . . .'

'Stop your prattling!' snapped the *Corregidor*, slapping Garduña's thieving hand. 'My predecessor was an idiot to have you as his constable! But let's get on with the important business. You just said that Lucas's mill is officially inside the boundaries of the next village and not this town . . . are you sure of it?'

'Positive! The jurisdiction of the city stops at that sandy ravine where I was sitting this afternoon waiting for Your Honour . . . Christ! if I'd been in your place . . .'

'Shut up!' shouted Don Eugenio. 'You're insolent!'

And he took half a sheet of paper, wrote a note, folded over one corner and gave it to Garduña.

'Here is,' he said as he gave him the note, 'the letter which you asked me for to hand to the mayor of that place. You will explain to him word for word everything he has to do. You can see how I'm following your plan to the letter! God help you if you get me into a mess!'

'No need to worry,' answered Garduña, 'Señor Juan López has a lot to be afraid of and when he sees Your Honour's signature he'll do everything I tell him; he owes at least a thousand *fanegas* of wheat to the royal storehouses and another thousand to the church storehouse and the last against all right, because he's not a widow or some poor farmer who is entitled to borrow without paying back interest or a surcharge. He's a gambler, a drunkard and lowlife and he's after the women so much that the whole village is up in arms. And that man is in a position of authority! Well, that's how things are in this country!'

'I told you to shut up! You're putting me off!' bellowed the *Corregidor*. 'Now let's get to the point,' he went on, changing his tone. 'It's a quarter past seven. The first thing you must do is go to my house and tell your mistress not to expect me for supper, and not wait up for me. Tell her I'll be working tonight until the curfew bell, and after that I'm going out on a secret patrol with you to see if we can catch some criminals. What I mean is . . . pull the wool over her eyes properly so she goes to bed without worrying. As you go, tell another constable to bring me some supper. I don't dare go home to my wife tonight because she knows me so well she can read my thoughts. Tell the cook to give you some of the honey fritters she made today and tell Juanete to be careful that nobody sees him and bring me half a pint of white wine from the tavern. When you've done that, go to the village straight-away and you should easily be there by half past eight!'

'I'll be there at eight o'clock prompt!' exclaimed Garduña.

'Don't contradict me!' roared the *Corregidor*, remembering his position again.

Garduña bowed.

'So, we were saying,' the former went on, returning to his human condition, 'that at eight o'clock prompt you'll be in the village. From the village to the mill must be about . . . I think, half a league . . .'

'A short one.'

'Don't interrupt!'

The constable bowed again.

'Short,' went on the *Corregidor*. 'So, do you think that at ten o'clock . . .?'

'Before ten! By half past nine you can knock at the mill door without need to worry!'

'Listen! Don't tell me what I have to do! Of course you'll be . . .'

'I'll be everywhere . . . but my headquarters will be the sandy ravine near the mill. Oh yes, I was forgetting. Go on foot and don't carry a lantern . . .'

'I don't need your blasted advice! D'you think its the first time I've been out on a campaign?'

'Sorry, sir. Ah! Something else. Don't knock at the big door which faces the little square with the climbing vine. Knock at the little door over the mill-race.'

'There's another door over the mill-race? Now there's something that I'd never thought of!'

'Yes, sir. That little door opens right on to the miller and his wife's bedroom. And Lucas doesn't go in or out through it, so that, even if he came back unexpectedly . . .'

'Yes, yes, I understand . . . don't confuse me any more!'

'Finally, I think Your Honour should try to get well away before dawn. It gets light at six these days . . .'

'That's another useless piece of advice! I'll be home by five. But that's enough talk. Go on, clear off out of it!'

'Well sir, good luck, then,' exclaimed the constable, stretching out his hand sideways to the *Corregidor* and looking at the ceiling as he did so.

The *Corregidor* put a peseta into that hand and Garduña disappeared as if by magic.

'Oh Lord,' sighed the old man in a minute, 'I forgot to tell that windbag to bring me a pack of cards as well. I could have amused myself until half past nine seeing if I could finish that *solitaire*.'

CHAPTER 15

A Prosaic Farewell

It must have been about nine that same night. Lucas and Señora Frasquita had finished all the work in the mill and the domestic chores, and supped on an endive salad, a pound or so of stewed meat and tomatoes and a few of the grapes left in the aforementioned basket. They washed it all down with a little wine and loud laughter at the expense of the *Corregidor*. Then husband and wife looked at each other lovingly, content with the world and themselves, saying, with a couple of yawns which revealed all the peace and tranquillity of their hearts:

'Now then, to bed, and we'll see what tomorrow brings.'

At that moment two loud and impatient knocks were heard at the front door of the mill.

Husband and wife looked at each other, startled.

It was the first time anybody had knocked at their door at that time of the night.

'I'll go and see,' said the fearless Navarrese woman, making for the courtyard.

'No, stop! That's my job!' exclaimed Lucas with such pride and authority that Señora Frasquita let him go. 'I told you not to go out!' he added sternly, seeing that his obstinate wife was intending to follow him.

She obeyed and stayed inside the house.

'Who is it?' asked Lucas from inside the gate.

'The Law,' answered a voice from the other side of the gate.

'What Law?'

'The Law of the village! Open to His Worship the Mayor!'

Meanwhile Lucas had put his eye to a cleverly disguised little spyhole in the gate and, recognizing in the moonlight the rustic constable of the next village:

'You mean I should open to the drunkard of a constable,' retorted the miller, pulling back the bar.

'It's all the same,' the man outside answered, 'since I've got a letter written by His Worship! A very good evening to you, Lucas,' he said, as he walked in, in a much less official, milder and quieter voice, as if he were already another man.

'Good evening to you, Toñuelo,' answered the Murcian. 'Let's see what that order's about. And Señor Juan López could find a much better time than this to send messages to decent people! Of course! It's your fault! I can see you now, you've been getting drunk at all the farms on the way. Would you like a drink?'

'No, Señor, I haven't got time for anything. You've got to come with me at once. Read the order.'

'What do you mean, go with you?' exclaimed Lucas, going into the mill after taking the piece of paper. 'Frasquita! Let's have a light here!'

Señora Frasquita put down something she had in her hand and took down the lamp.

Lucas glanced quickly at what his wife had put down and recognized his bell-mouth, that is, an enormous blunderbuss which took half-pound balls.

The miller glanced at his wife with gratitude and tenderness in his eyes and said, as he held her face:

'What a woman you are!'

Señora Frasquita, as pale and calm as a marble statue, raised the lamp which she held with two fingers without the least tremble in her wrist and answered curtly;

'Come on, read it.'

The order read thus:

In the name of H.M. the King our Lord, (whom God keep) I instruct Lucas Fernández, miller, of these parts, as soon as he receives this order, to present himself before me without any excuse or pretext, warning him that, as the matter is secret he may not advise anyone of it. All under the corresponding penalties in case of disobedience.

The Mayor Juan López

And there was a cross instead of a signature.

'Listen you, what's this, then?' Lucas asked the constable. 'What's this order all about?'

'I don't know,' answered the rustic, a man of about thirty, whose sharp and malicious features, like those of a thief or a murderer, did not inspire much confidence in his truthfulness. 'I think it's to find out something about witchcraft or forged money ... but it's not you they're after ... they're calling you as a witness or an expert. I mean I haven't much idea what it's all about. Señor López will explain it in more detail.'

'Right!' exclaimed the miller. 'Tell him I'll come tomorrow.'

'Oh no, Señor. You've got to come straightaway, without a minute's delay. That is the order His Worship the Mayor gave me.'

There was a moment's silence.

Señora Frasquita's eyes flashed in anger.

Lucas kept his fixed on the ground, as if he were looking for something.

'But at least you'll give me time,' he exclaimed at last looking up, 'to go to the stable and saddle the donkey.'

'To hell with the donkey!' retorted the constable. 'Anybody can walk half a league! It's a nice night and there's a moon . . .'

'Yes, I can see it has risen . . . but my feet are badly swollen.'

'Well, let's not waste time then. I'll help you to saddle the donkey.'

'Eh? What? Are you afraid I'll run away?'

'I'm not afraid of anything, Lucas,' replied Toñuelo in the cold voice of a soulless man. 'I am the Law.'

And, as he spoke, he stood easy, which allowed him to reveal the short musket he held beneath his greatcoat.

'Look, Toñuelo, since you're going to the stable . . . to practise your proper trade . . . kindly saddle the other donkey as well,' said the miller's wife.

'What for?' asked the miller.

'For me! I'm going with you both.'

'No, you can't, Señora Frasquita,' objected the constable. 'My orders are to take your husband and that's all and to prevent you going after him. It's more than my job – and my neck – are worth. That's what I was told by Señor Juan López, so, off we go, Lucas.'

And he made towards the door.

'Very strange,' the miller said softly, without moving.

'Very strange indeed,' answered Señora Frasquita.

'It's something . . . I know . . .' Lucas went on muttering so that Toñuelo couldn't hear.

'Would you like me to go to town,' whispered Frasquita, 'and tell the *Corregidor* what's happening to us?'

'No!' Lucas said out aloud. 'Not that!'

'Well, what do you want me to do?' said the miller's wife forcefully.

'I want you . . . to look at me,' said the ex-soldier.

Husband and wife looked at each other without a word and

were so satisfied with the calm, resolute determination which their eyes communicated, that they ended by shrugging their shoulders and laughing.

Next, Lucas lit another lamp and went to the stable, saying mockingly to Toñuelo:

'Come on, friend, come and help me . . . if you would be so kind!'

Toñuelo followed him, humming a song in *sotto voce*.

A few minutes later Lucas left the mill riding a fine she-ass and followed by the constable.

The farewell of the couple had been merely . . .

'Make sure you lock up securely.'

'Wrap up, it's cold,' said Frasquita as she closed the door with lock, bar and bolt.

And that was all the farewell, kiss, embrace and parting look there was.

What need was there for more?

CHAPTER 16

Bird of Ill-Omen

LET us follow Lucas.

They had already travelled a quarter of a league without saying a word, the miller riding the ass and the constable goading it along with his staff of office, when, in front of them, at the top of a hill in the road, they spied an enormous bird approaching.

Its shadow was boldly outlined on the ground, brightly lit by the moon, drawn with such exactness that the miller exclaimed as soon as he saw it:

'Toñuelo, that's Garduña, with his three-cornered hat and his skinny legs!'

But before the other could reply, the shadow, doubtless wishing to avoid meeting them, had left the road and had broken into a run across country with the speed of a real weasel, thus living up to his name.

'I can't see anybody,' Toñuelo answered then, in the most natural tone imaginable.

'Nor can I,' replied Lucas, pretending all was normal.

And the suspicion that had already entered his mind began to grow and take on substance in the distrustful mind of the hump-backed miller.

'This trip of mine,' he said to himself, 'is a trick of the *Corregidor* to advance his love-plans.

'From the declaration of love I heard him make when I was up in the vine this afternoon I'm sure that old man from Madrid can't wait any more. There's no doubt about it; tonight he's going to pay a return visit to the mill and so he's begun by getting me out of the way ... but, so what if he has? Frasquita is Frasquita and she won't open the door even if they set fire to the house! No, even if she did open the door and even if, by some trick, the *Corregidor* did manage to surprise my marvellous Navarrese lass, the rascally old man would come off badly. Frasquita is Frasquita! All the same,' he added after a moment, 'it'd be best for me to get home tonight as quickly as I can.'

By then Lucas and the constable had arrived at the village and made their way to the Mayor's house.

CHAPTER 17

A Village Mayor

Señor Juan López, who as a private citizen and as Mayor was tyranny, ferocity and pride personified when he was dealing with those under him, condescended, nevertheless, at that time of night, after finishing official business, his farm affairs and administering the daily beating to his wife, to drink a pitcher of wine in the company of his Secretary and the Sacristan. They had been drinking for half the night already when the miller presented himself before the Mayor.

'Hullo there, Lucas!' he said, scratching his head to stimulate the deceitful side of his brain. 'How are you? Come on, Secretary, pour out a glass of wine for Lucas! And how's Frasquita? Still as pretty as ever. It's a long time since I last saw her! And I say, your milling's really good. The rye bread tastes like the finest flour! Well then, I say ... sit down and take the weight off your feet ... thank God we're in no hurry.'

'To the Devil with hurry, as far as I am concerned!' answered Lucas, who hadn't opened his mouth up to then but whose suspicions grew ever greater as he saw in what a friendly manner he was being received after such a terrible and urgent summons.

'Well now, Lucas,' continued the Mayor, 'since you're not in any great hurry, you'll sleep here tonight and we'll deal with our little matter early tomorrow morning.'

'That's a good idea,' answered Lucas with irony and hiding his feelings so well, that he was more than a match for Señor Juan López's diplomacy, 'since the matter's not urgent, I'll sleep away from home tonight.'

'It's not urgent, and you're in no trouble,' added the Mayor, deceived by the person he thought he was deceiving. 'You've nothing to worry about at all. Listen you, Toñuelo, draw up that half-bushel of hay and let Lucas have a seat!'

'Well then, give us another drink!' exclaimed the miller, sitting down.

'Have this!' replied the Mayor, handing him the full glass.

'It's in good hands ... drink the first half yourself.'

'Well then, your very good health!' said Señor Juan López, drinking half the glass.

'And yours ... Mr Mayor,' replied Lucas, finishing the other half.

'Here, Manuela,' shouted the village Mayor. 'Tell your mistress that Lucas is staying here tonight. Tell them to put a pillow down in the granary.'

'No, no, I won't allow it. I can sleep wonderfully in the straw.'

'But you know we've got pillows ...'

'Yes, of course. But what do you want to put your family to inconvenience for? I've got my topcoat ...'

'Well, Señor, as you will. Manuela! Tell your mistress not to put the pillow in the barn!'

'But what I will ask you,' went on Lucas, emitting a fearful yawn, 'is to let me go to bed at once. I had a lot of milling to do last night and I haven't shut my eyes since.'

'Granted!' replied the Mayor majestically. 'You may retire when you wish.'

'I think it's also time for all of us to retire,' said the Sacristan, looking into the wine pitcher to calculate how much was left. 'It must be about ten o'clock or nearly that.'

'A quarter to ten!,' exclaimed the Secretary, after sharing out the rest of that night's wine among their glasses.

'Right! To bed, gentlemen!' exclaimed the host, drinking his down.

'Good night, gentlemen,' added the miller, drinking his.

'Wait, they'll light your way . . . Toñuelo! Take Lucas to the barn!'

'This way, Lucas,' said Toñuelo, taking the jug away also, just in case there were a few drops of wine left.

'Good night, God be with you,' added the Sacristan, after draining all the glasses.

And off he went, staggering and singing the *de profundis* cheerfully.

'Well, now,' said the Mayor to the Secretary when they were alone. 'Lucas hasn't suspected anything. We can go to bed in peace and . . . the best of luck to the *Corregidor*!'

CHAPTER 18

Where Lucas is Seen to be a Very Light Sleeper

FIVE minutes later, a man climbed down from the window of His Worship the Mayor's barn, a window which looked over the farmyard and which wasn't four yards from the ground.

In the yard was a shed roof over a large set of stalls where there were six or seven horses of different breed tied up. All of them were females. The horses, mules and donkeys of the stronger sex were housed separately in another place close by.

The man untied his donkey, which was still saddled. He pulled back the bar and undid the bolt which held it. He opened the gate very carefully and found himself in the open country.

Once there, he mounted the ass, dug his heels in and departed like a flash of lightning for the city, but not by the ordinary route. He rode along sown fields and through gullies like someone anticipating a possibly unpleasant meeting.

It was Lucas, going to his mill.

CHAPTER 19

Voices Crying in the Desert

'SET mayors on me, would he? He'll soon see what a man from Archena does about that!' the Murcian said to himself as he rode along. 'Tomorrow morning I'll go and see the Bishop, just to be safe, and I'll tell him everything that has happened to me tonight. Fancy calling me with so much haste and secrecy, at such a strange time, telling me to come alone, talking about the King's business and forged money and witchcraft and goblins, and then giving me two glasses of wine and sending me off to bed! Well, I mean to say, it's crystal clear, Garduña brought those instructions to the village from the *Corregidor* and it's just about now that the *Corregidor*'s trying to make out with my wife. Who knows if I'll find him knocking at the door of the mill? Perhaps I'll find him inside already! Perhaps . . .! But what am I saying? How could I doubt Frasquita? It's a sin to do so. She couldn't . . . Frasquita couldn't possibly . . . couldn't? What am I saying? Is there anything impossible in the world? Didn't she marry me, though she was so beautiful and I was so ugly?'

And, making this last observation, the wretched humpback began to weep.

Then he stopped the donkey to calm down; he wiped his eyes, gave a deep sigh, took out his tobacco and smoking things, shredded the tobacco and rolled a black cigarette. Then he took the flint, tinder and steel and after a few attempts, managed to strike a light.

Just then he heard the sound of steps in the direction of the road, which was about three hundred yards away.

'How careless of me!' he said. 'Of course, the Law must be looking for me and I've given myself away by striking a light.'

So he hid the light and got down from the donkey, hiding himself carefully behind it.

But the donkey understood things differently and uttered a bray of pleasure.

'Damn you!' exclaimed Lucas, and tried to cover its mouth with his hand.

At the same time there was another bray on the road, in the way of a loving reply.

'I've had it!' the miller thought. 'The proverb's right, "Never have anything to do with animals".'

As he said this, he climbed back on the donkey, goaded it and charged off in the direction opposite to the one from where the second bray had come.

The odd thing was that the person riding on the animal which answered Lucas's donkey must have been as startled by Lucas as Lucas was by him. I say this because he also rode away from the road, doubtless suspecting that the other was a constable or a miscreant paid by Don Eugenio, and sped through the crops on the other side.

Meanwhile the Murcian was still going over his problems:

'What a night! What a world! What a life . . . in the last hour! Constables changed into pimps, mayors who conspire against my honour, donkeys who bray when there's no need and here, in my breast, a miserable heart which dared to doubt the noblest woman that God ever created! Oh God, God! Help me get home quickly and find my Frasquita!'

Lucas rode on, over crops and through thickets until at last, at about eleven o'clock that night, he reached the main door of the mill without incident.

Tragedy! The door of the mill was open!

CHAPTER 20

Doubt and Reality

IT was open. But, when he had left he had heard his wife lock, bar and bolt it!

So, nobody but his wife could have opened it!

But how? When? Why? Had she been tricked? Had she been given an order? Or had she opened the door deliberately and voluntarily, in virtue of a previous agreement with the *Corregidor*?

What was he about to see? What was he about to learn? What awaited him inside his house? Had Frasquita run away? Had she been abducted? Could she be dead? Or was she in the arms of his rival?

'The *Corregidor* counted on my not being able to get back at all tonight,' Lucas said to himself lugubriously. 'That village mayor probably had orders to go as far as putting me in chains rather than let me come back . . . Did Frasquita know all this? Was she in the plot? Or has she been the victim of deceit, violence and treachery?'

The unhappy man's distressing thoughts took no longer to be expressed than the time he took to walk through the little courtyard with the climbing vine.

The door of the house was also open; as in all country dwellings, the door opened directly on to the kitchen.

But an enormous fire was blazing in the hearth, a hearth which had been cold when he left and which was never lit until well into the month of December! To cap it all, a lighted oil lamp was hanging from one of the hooks on the kitchen rack.

What did it all mean? And how did all those signs of sitting up late and company go together with the deathly silence that reigned in the house?

What had become of his wife?

Then, and only then, Lucas noticed some clothes hanging

over the backs of two or three chairs arranged around the fireplace.

He stared at the clothes and uttered such a profound bellow that it stuck in his throat, emerging as a dull and suppressed sob.

The wretched man thought he was choking, and put his hands to his throat. His face was livid and convulsed, his eyes staring out of their orbits. He looked at those clothes, with the horror of the man about to be hanged who is presented with the execution garment.

Because what he saw there were the crimson cloak, the three-cornered hat, the coat, the light-blue waistcoat, the black silk breeches, the white stockings, the buckled shoes and even the staff, short sword and gloves of the execrable *Corregidor*. What he saw there was the garment of his ignominy, the shroud of his honour, the winding sheet of his good fortune!

The fearsome musket was still in the same corner where Frasquita had left it two hours earlier.

Lucas leapt like a tiger and seized it. He pushed the ramrod down the barrel and saw that it was loaded. He looked at the flint and found that it was in place.

Then he went back to the staircase which led to the room where for so many years he had slept with Frasquita, and muttered thickly:

'They are there.'

Then he took a step in that direction but at once he stopped to look around and see if anybody was watching him.

'Nobody,' he said to himself. 'Only God . . . and this is His will!'

Thus confirming the sentence, he was about to take another step when his eyes, looking right and left, noticed a folded sheet of paper on the table.

He saw it, fell on it and had it in his grip in less than a second.

That paper was the appointment of Frasquita's nephew, signed by Don Eugenio de Zúñiga y Ponce de León!

'That was the price of the sale!' thought Lucas as he

stuffed the paper in his mouth to stifle his shouts and give his rage something to feed on. 'I always suspected that she loved her family more than me! We didn't have children! That's the cause of it all!'

And the miserable man was on the point of beginning to weep again. But then his rage grew once more and he said, with a terrible expression on his face, though in a quieter voice.

'Upstairs! Upstairs!'

And he began to climb the stairs, creeping up on all fours, one hand resting on the staircase, and the other holding the musket, and with the infamous piece of paper between his teeth.

When he reached the bedroom door, which was closed, his logical suspicions were corroborated by the few rays of light which shone through the joints of the planks and the keyhole.

'There they are,' he said once again.

And he stopped for a moment as if to swallow that new draught of bitterness.

Then he climbed on, until he reached the door of the bedroom.

No sound came from inside.

'Perhaps there isn't anyone there,' hope whispered to him timidly.

But at that very moment the unfortunate man heard a cough from inside the room.

It was the half-asthmatic cough of the *Corregidor*!

No doubt about it! The drowning man could not even find a straw to clutch!

The miller grinned ghoulishly in the darkness. How could the flashes of anger in his eyes fail to shine out? What is all the lightning of storms compared with the blaze that burns sometimes in a man's heart?

Nevertheless Lucas – such was his nature, as has already been explained – began to calm down as soon as he heard his enemy's cough.

Reality hurt him less than doubt. As he had told Frasquita that very afternoon, from the exact moment when he lost the only faith that maintained him, he began to change into a new man.

Just like the Moor of Venice – with whom we compared him previously when we described his character – disillusion killed all the love in his heart in one blow, changing as it did so the nature of his spirit and making the world appear to him as a strange place where he had just arrived. The only difference was that by nature Lucas was less tragic, less austere and more selfish than the crazed killer of Desdemona.

It is a strange phenomenon, but natural to such situations. Doubt, or hope, which was one and the same thing in this case, returned once more to torment him.

'What if I were wrong?' he thought. 'What if it was Frasquita who coughed?'

In the trials of his misfortune, he forgot he had seen the *Corregidor*'s clothes by the fireplace, that he had found the door of the mill open, that he had read the document proving the infamy.

So he stooped and applied his eye to the keyhole, trembling with doubt and emotion.

His view could only take in a small triangle of bed, near the head. But just in that little triangle appeared one end of the pillows and on the pillows, the *Corregidor*'s head!

The miller's face contracted grotesquely in another hellish grin.

It was as if he were happy again.

'Now I know the worst! I must think,' he murmured as he stood up calmly.

And he descended the staircase with the same cautiousness with which he had climbed it.

'It's very tricky ... I must think. I've got more than enough time for everything,' he thought as he went down.

When he reached the kitchen, he sat down in the middle of the room and buried his head in his hands.

He remained in this position for a long time until he was awakened from his reverie by a gentle tap on one foot.

It was the musket, which had slipped off his knees and was signalling its presence by that tap.

'No, I said no!' muttered Lucas, looking straight at the weapon. 'You're no use! Everybody would be sorry for them . . . and I'd be hanged. He's a *Corregidor*, and killing a *Corregidor* is still an unpardonable offence in Spain. They'll say I killed him out of unprovoked jealousy and that I undressed him afterwards and put him in my bed. They'll also say that I killed my wife on mere suspicion. And they'd hang me! Besides, I'd not be seen to have much spirit or brains if everybody were sorry for me when my life was put to an end. They'd all laugh at me! They'd say that my cuckolding is very natural, since I am a hunchback and Frasquita is so pretty! No, not at all! What I must do is get revenge and, when I have it, triumph over him, despise him, laugh, laugh and laugh, laugh at everyone. In that way I can stop anybody taking advantage again of this hump which I have managed to make almost an object of envy and which would be so grotesque on a gallows!'

Such were the thoughts, spoken aloud, of Lucas, though perhaps he didn't realize everything he was saying. As a result of them, he put the musket back in its place and began to walk with his arms behind his back and his head low, as if seeking his revenge in the ground, in the earth, in the wretchedness of life, in some ignominious and ridiculous practical joke on his wife and the *Corregidor*, far from seeking his revenge in justice, in a challenge, in heaven . . . as any other man, in his place, would have done if he were less rebellious to any law of nature, of society or his own feelings.

Suddenly, his eyes fell on the *Corregidor*'s clothes.

Then he stopped dead in his tracks.

And then, little by little his face began to show indefinable happiness, joy and triumph . . . until at last he began to laugh in great guffaws, but with no sound, so that they shouldn't hear him above. He pressed his fists into his sides so as not to burst, trembling all over like an epileptic and being obliged in the end to collapse into a chair until that convulsion of sarcastic rejoicing had passed.

It was Mephistopheles himself laughing.

As soon as he grew calm again, he began to undress with

feverish haste. He put all his clothes on the same chairs which the *Corregidor*'s apparel occupied. He put on all the latter's garments, from his buckled shoes to his three-cornered hat. He girded on the sword, wrapped himself in the crimson cloak, took the stick and the gloves and, leaving the mill, walked towards the town, swaying just like Don Eugenio de Zúñiga and repeating from time to time this sentence which expressed his thoughts in a nutshell:

'The *Corregidor*'s wife is beautiful also!'

CHAPTER 21

On Guard, Sir!

LET us leave Lucas for a moment and discover what had really happened in the mill since we left Frasquita there alone until her husband returned and discovered such shattering changes.

It was about an hour after Lucas had departed with Toñuelo when Frasquita, who was very upset and had sworn not to go to bed until her husband returned, and was knitting in the bedroom in the upper storey of the house, heard pitiful cries from outside, coming from the place not very far away where the mill-race water flowed.

'Help, help, I'm drowning! Frasquita, Frasquita!' cried a man's voice, in the despairing tones of hopelessness.

'Could that be Lucas?' she thought, filled with a dread that there is no need to describe.

In the bedroom itself there was a little door, already mentioned by Garduña, which did in fact look on to the upper part of the mill-race. Señora Frasquita opened it unhesitatingly, in spite of the fact that she didn't recognize the voice which craved help, and found herself face to face with the *Corregidor*, who at that moment emerged dripping from the swift-flowing channel.

'God help me! God help me!' stammered the infamous old man. 'I thought I was going to drown.'

'What? Is it you? What does this mean? How dare you? What are you doing here at this time of night?' cried the miller's wife with more indignation than fright, but automatically moving back.

'Quiet, woman, be quiet,' stuttered the *Corregidor*, slipping into the room behind her. 'I'll tell you everything. I was near to drowning. The water pulled me along like a feather. Look, look at the state I'm in.'

'Out, get out of here!' retorted Señora Frasquita more harshly. 'You don't have to explain anything to me. I understand it all only too well. What do I care if you get drowned? Did I ask you to come? What a shameful thing to do! That's why you had my husband arrested!'

'Listen, woman.'

'I won't listen. Go away at once, Señor *Corregidor*. Go away or I won't be responsible for your life!'

'What's that?'

'You heard me! My husband's not at home. But I am quite capable of making you respect me myself. Go the way you came, unless you want me to throw you back into the water with my own hands!'

'Now, now, my girl, don't shout so much. I'm not deaf,' exclaimed the old libertine. 'If I'm here, it's for a reason. I've come to release Lucas, whom a village mayor arrested by mistake. But, before anything else, you must dry my clothes. I'm soaked to the skin.'

'I'm telling you to go away!'

'Be quiet, you silly girl! What do you know? Look, I've brought you the appointment for your nephew ... light the lamp and we can talk. And, while my clothes are drying, I'll get into that bed.'

'Oh, yes? So you admit you came for me? So you admit that you had my Lucas arrested for that reason? So you brought the appointment and everything, did you? – Heavens alive! What did this old fool think I was!'

'Frasquita! I am the *Corregidor*!'

'I don't care if you are the King himself! You have no control over me! I am my husband's wife and the mistress of my house. Do you think I'm scared of *corregidors*? I can go to Madrid, and the ends of the earth, if I have to, to ask for justice against an insolent old man who uses his prestige for such base ends. And, what's more, tomorrow I can put on my *mantilla* and go and see your lady wife!'

'You won't do anything of the sort,' answered the *Corregidor*, losing his patience and changing his approach. 'You won't do anything of the sort because I'll shoot you if I see you won't listen to reason . . .'

'Shoot me!' exclaimed Frasquita, in a low voice.

'Yes ,shoot you . . . and there won't be any consequences for me because I've spread it around in town that I'm after some criminals tonight. So don't be silly, love me, as I adore you!'

'Señor *Corregidor*, shoot me?' Frasquita repeated, throwing her arms back and her body forward as if to throw herself on her adversary.

'If you keep on, I shall shoot you and so I'll be free of your threats and your beauty,' answered the *Corregidor*, full of fear and taking out a pair of pocket pistols.

'So you've got pistols as well? And in your other pocket my nephew's appointment,' said Frasquita, nodding her head. 'Well sir, the choice is easy enough. Wait a minute, Your Worship, I'm going to light the lamp.'

And as she spoke she hastened to the staircase and leapt down its three steps.

The *Corregidor* picked up the lamp and left the room behind the miller's wife, fearful she was going to escape. But he had to go down the stairs much more slowly. The result was that, when he reached the kitchen he collided with Frasquita who was already coming back to meet him.

'So you said you were going to shoot me did you?' exclaimed that fearless woman stepping back. 'Right then, on guard sir, for I'm ready for you!'

And as she spoke she took aim with the formidable musket which plays such an important part in this story.

'Stop, stop, wretched woman! What are you going to do?' cried the *Corregidor*, half-dead with fright. 'What I said about shooting you was only a joke. Look . . . the pistols aren't loaded. But the news about the appointment for your nephew is true. Here it is ... take it ... its a present ... it's yours!'

And, trembling, he placed it on the table.

'That's a good place for it!' retorted the Navarrese woman, 'I'll use it tomorrow to light the stove when I cook my husband's breakfast. I don't want anything from you, not even favours. And if my nephew ever comes from Estella, it'll be to spit on your ugly hand with which you wrote out his name on that revolting piece of paper. Right, that's enough said! Leave my house! Come on, come on, quick! I've got the scent of gunpowder in my nostrils already!'

The *Corregidor* did not reply to this speech. He had grown deathly pale, almost blue. His eyes were twisted and a tremble had taken control of his whole body as if he were suffering from a tertian ague. Finally his teeth began to chatter and he fell to the ground, victim of a frightening convulsion.

The alarm of falling into the water, his soaking-wet clothes, the violent scene in the bedroom and the fear of the musket with which Frasquita was threatening him had exhausted all the strength of the sickly old man.

'I'm dying,' he stammered. 'Call Garduña! Call Garduña, he's out there, in the ravine. I mustn't die in this house!'

He could not go on. He shut his eyes and lay there as if dead.

'And he'll die as he says,' Frasquita exclaimed. 'But, my God, this is terrible. What shall I do with this man in my house? What will people say about me if he dies? What will Lucas say? How could I excuse myself since it was I who opened the door for him? Oh no, I mustn't stay here with him. I must find my husband. I'll scandalize everybody rather than lose my honour!'

Having made up her mind, she put down the musket, went to the farmyard, took the one donkey still there, saddled it as best she could, opened the large gate in the fence, leapt on it in one movement in spite of her plump build and rode out to the sandy ravine.

'Garduña! Garduña!' she cried as she approached the place.

'Here,' replied the constable soon, appearing from behind a bush. 'Is it you, Señora Frasquita?'

'Yes, it's me. Go to the mill and look after your master, for he's dying.'

'What are you talking about? What sort of a trick is this?'

'It's the truth, Garduña.'

'And what about you, darling? Where are you going at this time of night?'

'Me? Get out of my way, you idiot! I'm going to town for a doctor,' answered Frasquita, goading the donkey with a kick of her heel and Garduña with a kick from her toe.

And she took the road not to the city, as she had just said, but to the near-by village.

Garduña didn't notice that, because he was already striding towards the mill and saying to himself as he went:

'She's going for a doctor! She can't do anything else, poor girl! But he's not much of a man. What a time to be ill! God gives things when you're too old to enjoy them.'

CHAPTER 22

Garduña Gets Moving

WHEN Garduña reached the mill, the *Corregidor* was beginning to recover consciousness and trying to stand up.

Next to him, also lying on the floor, was the lighted lamp which His Honour had brought down from the bedroom.

'Has she gone already?' was Don Eugenio's first sentence.

'Who?'

'The Devil . . . I mean, the miller's wife.'

'Yes, Señor, she's gone . . . and I don't think she went in a very good mood.'

'Ay, Garduña, I'm dying!'

'But what's Your Worship saying . . . for God's sake!'

'I fell in the mill-race and I'm soaked to the skin. I'm frozen to the marrow.'

'Oh, now. That's the story, is it?'

'Garduña, have a care what you say!'

'I'm not saying anything, Señor.'

'Very well then. Get me out of this mess.'

'At once . . . I'll show Your Worship how quickly I can put everything straight.'

Those were the constable's words and, in two shakes of a lamb's tail he took the light with one hand and tucked the *Corregidor* under his arm with the other. He took him up to the bedroom, took all his clothes off, put him into bed, ran to the wine-press, gathered an armful of wood, went to the kitchen, made a large fire, brought down all his master's clothes, placed them over the backs of two or three chairs, lit an oil lamp, hung it from the kitchen rack and went up to the bedroom again.

'How are we, then?' he asked Don Eugenio, lifting the lamp so as to get a better view of his face.

'Marvellous! I know I'm going to sweat. I'll hang you tomorrow, Gardŭna.'

'Why, Señor?'

'And you have the gall to ask me why? When I followed the plan you made for me do you think I was expecting to find myself alone in this bed after being baptized – by total immersion – a second time? I'm going to hang you tomorrow without fail!'

'But please, won't Your Worship tell me something . . . Señora Frasquita?'

'Señora Frasquita tried to murder me. That's all I got from your advice. I tell you I'll hang you tomorrow morning!'

'It can't be so bad, Señor *Corregidor*,' replied the constable.

'Why do you say that, you insolent dog? Because you can see I'm flat on my back here?'

'No Señor. I said that because Señora Frasquita could not have behaved so inhumanly as Your Worship says, considering she's gone to town to fetch a doctor for you . . .'

'Oh Lord! Are you sure she's gone to the city?' exclaimed Don Eugenio, more alarmed than ever.

'Well, at least that's what she told me.'

'Run, Garduña, run. Oh, that's the end for me. D'you know why Señora Frasquita's gone to the city? To tell the whole story to my wife! To tell her that I'm here! Oh my God, my

God! How could I have thought this would happen? I thought she'd have gone to the village for her husband. I've got him safely guarded there so it didn't worry me. But if she went to the city? Hurry, Garduña, Hurry. You're a great walker. Save me! Stop that dreadful miller's wife going into my house!'

'And Your Honour won't hang me if I manage to?' asked the constable ironically.

'On the contrary! I'll give you some shoes in very good condition that are too big for me! I'll give you everything you want!'

'Right, I'm on my way. You can sleep peacefully. I'll be back here in half an hour after I leave the Navarrese woman in the prison. They don't say I'm faster than a she-ass for nothing!' said Garduña as he disappeared down the stairs.

It goes without saying that it was while the constable was away that the miller was in the mill and saw visions through the keyhole.

So, let us leave the *Corregidor* sweating in a strange bed and Garduña running to the city (whither he would soon be followed by Lucas wearing the three-cornered hat and the crimson cloak) and, putting our best foot forward also, let us hasten towards the village, following the valiant Señora Frasquita.

CHAPTER 23

Once More the Desert and the Well-Known Voices

THE only adventure that Frasquita had on her journey from the mill to the village was a scare when she saw somebody lighting tinder in the middle of a planted field.

'Could it be one of the *Corregidor*'s agents? Is he coming to arrest me?' thought the miller's wife.

At that moment she heard a bray from the same direction.

'Donkeys out at this time of night?' thought Señora

Frasquita. 'But there's no market-garden or farm round here ... The spirits are certainly having a fine time tonight! It certainly can't be my husband's donkey. What could my Lucas be doing at midnight, stopping off the road. No, no, it must be a spy!'

The donkey that Señora Frasquita rode also thought it would be a good idea to bray just at that moment.

'Shut up, devil take you!' she said, pushing a pin right into its withers.

And, fearing a most inconvenient encounter, she also rode her mount off the road and made it trot through the sown fields.

The rest of her journey was uneventful and she arrived at the first houses of the village at about eleven o'clock that night.

CHAPTER 24

A King of that Time

THE Mayor was sleeping heavily, back to back with his wife so that the pair formed the figure of the Austrian double eagle mentioned by our immortal Quevedo, when Toñuelo knocked at the door of the nuptial bedroom and informed Señor Juan López that Señora Frasquita, of the mill, wished to speak to him.

There is no need to recount all the grumbling and oaths which inevitably accompanied the act of awaking and dressing for the village Mayor, so we shall move on at once to the moment when the miller's wife saw him come, stretching like a gymnast limbering up and exclaiming in the midst of an endless yawn:

'A very good evening to you, Señora Frasquita! What brings you this way? Didn't Toñuelo tell you to stay in the mill? Are you disobeying my authority?'

'I have to see my Lucas!' she replied, 'I must see him immediately! Tell your men to tell him his wife is here!'

' "*I have to? I must?*" Señora, you forget you are speaking to the King.'

'Oh, leave off about kings, Señor Juan, I'm not in the mood for joking. You know only too well what's happening to me. You know only too well why you arrested my husband!'

'I know nothing, Señora Frasquita ... and, as for your husband, he's not arrested, just sleeping peacefully as a guest in my house and treated as I treat decent people. Here, Toñuelo! Toñuelo! Go to the barn and tell Lucas to wake up and run along here. Now, tell me what's going on. Were you afraid to sleep alone?'

'Don't be a hypocrite, Señor Juan. You know very well that I don't like your jokes and I don't care very much for what you do when you're serious either! What's happened is very simple. You and the *Corregidor* wanted to ruin me but you've both come out of it with bloody noses. I'm here without anything to be ashamed of and the Señor *Corregidor*'s at the mill dying!'

'The *Corregidor* dying!' exclaimed his subordinate. 'Señora, d'you know what you are saying?'

'Just what you heard. He fell in the mill-race and nearly drowned, or he's caught pneumonia or something or other. Let the *Corregidor*'s wife worry about that. I've come to get my husband and I reserve my right to set off for Madrid tomorrow and tell the King ....'

'Hell, the Devil! You, Manuela! Go and saddle the mule for me. Señora Frasquita, I'm off to the mill. Heaven help you if you've hurt the Señor *Corregidor*!'

'Your Worship, Your Worship,' exclaimed Toñuelo, as he came in looking more dead than alive. 'Lucas isn't in the barn. His donkey isn't in its stall either and the farmyard gate is open. The bird has flown!'

'What are you saying?' shouted Señor Juan López.

'Holy Mother of God! What's going to happen at my home!' exclaimed Señora Frasquita, 'Come on, quickly, Mr Mayor, let's waste no time! My husband will kill the *Corregidor* when he finds him there at this time of night!'

'So you think Lucas is at the mill?'

'Yes, of course I do. And here's something else. While I was on my way here I passed him without knowing who it was. He must have been the man who was lighting tinder in the middle of the field. Oh my God! When one thinks that animals have more sense than human beings! Because, Señor Juan, I can tell you that each of two donkeys knew the other was there and greeted each other, while Lucas and I didn't greet or even recognize each other . . . on the contrary we ran away and each assumed the other was a spy!'

'Your Lucas is in a fine mess,' retorted the Mayor. 'Now then, let's go and we'll see what we can do with all of you. Don't think you can play around with me. I am the King! But not a king like the one we have in Madrid now, or rather in the palace at El Pardo,* but more like the one who lived in Seville and was known as Don Pedro the Cruel. Here, Manuela! Bring me my staff of office and tell your mistress I'm going.'

The servant, who was certainly a better-looking girl than was comfortable for the Mayor's wife or for his morals, obeyed, and, as the mule was already saddled, Señora Frasquita and he rode off to the mill, followed by the indispensable Toñuelo.

CHAPTER 25

Garduña's Star

LET us go ahead of them, since we have the privilege of being able to travel faster than anyone.

Garduña was already back at the mill, after having looked for Señora Frasquita everywhere in the city.

The astute constable called in at the *Corregidor*'s offices on his way and found everything very calm. The doors were still open as during the day, which is the custom when the

* A town and palace situated a few miles north-west of Madrid, which was the winter residence of the Kings of Spain and later the permanent residence of General Franco.

Corregidor is out exercising his sacred functions. On the landing and in the reception room other constables and functionaries were drowsing unhurriedly awaiting their master. But, when they heard Garduña, two or three of them roused themselves and asked their leader and immediate superior:

'Is His Lordship coming now?'

'Nowhere near the place! Take it easy! I've come to ask if anything's been happening round here.'

'No, nothing.'

'What about My Lady?'

'In her private apartments.'

'Didn't a woman come through these doors a short while back?'

'Nobody's been here all night.'

'Well, don't let anybody in, whoever it is and whatever they say. Absolutely not. If the morning star comes and asks about His Worship or Madam, arrest it and put it in gaol!'

'Looks like they're after big fish tonight!' observed one of the *Corregidor*'s agents.

'Big game,' added another.

'The biggest!' replied Garduña in solemn tones. 'You'll see how delicate the question is when I tell you that the *Corregidor* and I are flushing out the suspect ourselves ... so ... I'll be seeing you, boys! Keep your eyes peeled!'

'*Vaya usted con Dios*, Señor Bastián,' they all replied as they saluted him.

'I'm slipping,' muttered Garduña as he left the *Corregidor*'s offices. 'Even women can trick me! The miller's wife went to the village to look for her husband and not to the city ... Poor Garduña! Where's your sharp nose gone?'

And with these words he made for the mill.

The constable was right to regret the loss of his fine nose, because he didn't scent a man who was hiding behind some osiers, close to the sandy ravine outside the mill, who exclaimed into his cloak, or rather the *Corregidor*'s crimson cloak:

'Careful, now, here comes Garduña. He'd better not see me!'

It was Lucas, dressed as the *Corregidor*, on his way to the city, repeating every now and then his diabolical sentence:

73

'The *Corregidor*'s wife is pretty too!'

Garduña walked past without seeing him and the false *Corregidor* left his hiding place and entered the town. Shortly afterwards the constable reached the mill, as we said.

CHAPTER 26

Reaction

THE *Corregidor* was still in bed, just as Lucas had seen him through the keyhole.

'I'm having a marvellous sweat, Garduña. I've just escaped an illness,' he exclaimed as soon as the constable entered the room. 'What about Señora Frasquita? Did you find her? Is she with you? Has she talked to Madam?'

'The miller's wife, Señor,' replied Garduña in tones of anguish, 'tricked me like some poor devil, for she did not go to the city. She went to the village . . . to get her husband. I beg Your Honour to pardon my stupidity.'

'Better, better still,' said the *Corregidor* from Madrid as his eyes glittered with evil. 'Everything's saved then. Before dawn, Lucas and Señora Frasquita will be on their way to the Inquisition's prisons, tied together, and there they'll rot without anyone to whom they can recount tonight's adventures. Bring me my clothes, Garduña, they'll be dry by now. Bring them and dress me. The lover is about to change into the *Corregidor*!'

Garduña went down to the kitchen for the clothes.

CHAPTER 27

Rally to the King!

MEANWHILE, Señora Frasquita, Señor Juan López and Toñuelo were approaching the mill, where they arrived soon afterwards.

'I'll go in first!' exclaimed the Mayor of the village. 'That's why I'm in charge around here! Follow me, Toñuelo, Señora Frasquita, wait at the door until I call you!'

So Señor Juan López went in, under the climbing vine where, in the moonlight he saw a man who was almost hunchbacked, dressed like the miller, in a waistcoat and breeches of dun-coloured corduroy, a black sash, blue stockings, a round Murcian plush hat and his cloak over his shoulders.

'That's him!' shouted the Mayor. 'Give yourself up, Lucas!'

The man in the plush hat tried to go back into the mill.

'Surrender!' shouted Toñuelo in his turn, jumping on him, grabbing him by the neck, digging his knee into his spine and throwing him to the ground.

At the same time another fury leaped on Toñuelo, grasping him around the waist, threw him on the paved floor and began to set about him

It was Señora Frasquita, shouting:

'You swine! Leave my Lucas alone!'

But, at that moment, somebody else, who had appeared on the scene pulling a donkey with his right hand, pushed himself determinedly between the two and tried to protect Toñuelo.

It was Garduña who, taking the village mayor for Don Eugenio de Zúñiga, said to the miller's wife:

'Señora, have some respect for my master.'

And he knocked her flat on her back on top of the village bumpkin.

When Señora Frasquita saw herself caught between two fires, she kicked Garduña backwards in the pit of his stomach with such force that he fell down and measured his full length on the ground.

And now there were four people rolling over the floor.

Meanwhile Señor Juan López was preventing the man he assumed was Lucas from getting up, by keeping his foot in the small of his back.

'Garduña! Help! Rally to the King! I am the *Corregidor*!'

shouted Don Eugenio at length, feeling that the mayor's hoof, shod with rawhide sandals, was literally crushing him.

'The *Corregidor*! Yes, it's true!' said the astonished Señor Juan López.

'The *Corregidor*!' they all repeated.

And soon the four sprawling bodies were on their feet.

'Everybody to gaol!' cried Don Eugenio de Zúñiga. 'Everybody to the gallows!'

'But, Señor,' remarked Señor Juan López, falling on his knees. 'I beg Your Honour's pardon for having laid hands on you! How could I recognize Your Honour in such common dress?'

'Imbecile!' retorted the *Corregidor*. 'I had to put something on. Don't you know my clothes were stolen? Don't you know that a band of thieves, led by Lucas . . .?'

'It's a lie,' cried the Navarrese woman.

'Listen to me, Señora Frasquita,' said Garduña, drawing her aside, 'If the Señor *Corregidor* and company will excuse me, if you don't do something, we'll all be hanged, beginning with Lucas!'

'Why? What's the matter?' asked Señora Frasquita.

'Lucas is right now walking around the city dressed as the *Corregidor* and he might for all we know, have already reached My Lady's bedroom . . . in his disguise.'

And in a few words the constable brought her up to date about everything that had happened.

'Oh my God!' exclaimed the miller's wife. 'So my husband thinks I've been dishonoured! So he's gone to the city to get revenge! Come on, let's go to the city and show Lucas that he's wrong about me!'

'Let's go to the city and stop that man talking to my wife and telling her all the idiotic things he can have imagined!' said the *Corregidor*, going to one of the donkeys. 'Give me a leg up, Señor Mayor!'

'Yes, let's go to the city,' added Garduña, 'and please God, Señor *Corregidor*, that Lucas, aided as he is by your clothes, has contented himself with just speaking to Madam!'

'What's that you say, you wretch?' interrupted Don

Eugenio de Zúñiga. 'Do you think that peasant is capable . . . ?'

'. . . of everything!' answered Señora Frasquita.

CHAPTER 28

'Ave Maria Purisima!
Half Past Twelve and All's Well!'

THE night watchman was uttering these cries through the streets of the city when the miller's wife and the *Corregidor*, each on one of the mill donkeys, Señor Juan López on his mule and the two constables on foot, reached the door of the *Corregidor*'s residence.

The door was shut.

It appeared that everything was over for the day, both for the administrator and the administered.

'A bad sign,' thought Garduña. And he rapped on the door with the knocker, two or three times.

A long time passed and nobody answered or came to the door.

Señora Frasquita's countenance had turned a sickly yellow.

The *Corregidor* had already eaten all the finger-nails on both his hands.

Nobody said a word.

Bang! Bang! Bang! Blows and yet more blows on the door of the *Corregidor*'s residence, delivered in turn by the two constables and by Señor Juan López. Nothing! Nobody replied! Nobody came to open! There wasn't a sound to be heard!

All they could hear was the pure murmur of the fountain in the courtyard of the house.

And so the minutes passed, each an aeon of time.

At last, close on one o'clock, a little window on the third floor opened and a woman's voice said:

'Who's there?'

'It's the wet-nurse,' muttered Garduña.

'It's me,' answered Don Eugenio de Zúñiga. 'Open the door.'

There was a moment of silence.

'And who are you?' answered the nurse sharply.

'Well, can't you hear me? I'm the master, the *Corregidor*!'

A pause.

'Get along now then,' answered the good woman. 'My master came back an hour ago and went to bed at once. Go to bed, all of you, and sleep off all that wine you must have inside you!'

And the window was shut with a bang. Señora Frasquita buried her face in her hands.

'Nurse!' thundered the *Corregidor*, beside himself with rage. 'Didn't you hear me tell you to open the door? Can't you hear it's me? Do you want me to hang you as well?'

The window was reopened.

'Now look here,' protested the nurse, 'who do you think you are, shouting like that?'

'I am the *Corregidor*!'

'Don't lie again! Haven't I told you that the Señor *Corregidor* came in before twelve o'clock ... and with my own eyes I saw him go into My Lady's rooms? I suppose you want to amuse yourself at my expense. Well, you just wait and see what happens to you!'

At the same time the door opened suddenly and a swarm of servants and tipstaffs, each with a cudgel in his hands, hurled themselves on the people outside as they shouted in their rage:

'All right, where's the one who says he's the *Corregidor*? Where's the joker? Where's that drunken wretch?'

And an almighty row broke out in the darkness. Nobody could get things straight and the *Corregidor*, Garduña, Señor Juan López and Toñuelo didn't escape a few blows.

That was the second beating that the night's adventure had cost Don Eugenio, as well as the soaking he received in the mill-race.

Señora Frasquita stood aside from the melée and wept for the first time in her life.

'Lucas, Lucas,' she said. 'How could you doubt me? How could you hold another woman in your arms? Oh! Our misfortune has no remedy now!'

CHAPTER 29

Calm after the Storm

'WHAT is this disturbance?' At last, a tranquil, majestic and delicately toned voice echoed over the din.

They all looked up and saw a woman dressed in black, standing on the central balcony of the building.

'My Lady!' uttered the servants, suspending the tattoo they were playing with their cudgels.

'My wife,' stuttered Don Eugenio.

'Let those folk come in ... the Señor *Corregidor* says he will permit it ...' added the *Corregidor*'s wife.

The servants stood back and Señor de Zúñiga and his company entered the door and went upstairs.

No condemned man has ever walked up to the gallows with a step so trembling and a face so livid as the *Corregidor* walked up the stairs of his house. Nevertheless the thought that he might have been dishonoured was now beginning to stand out, noble egoist that he was, above all the misfortune he had caused, and which was affecting him, and above all the rest of the ridiculous situation in which he now found himself ...

'The most important thing is ...' he thought as he climbed the stairs, 'that I am a Zúñiga and a Ponce de León. Woe to those who have forgotten it! Woe to my wife if she has blotted the purity of my family name!'

CHAPTER 30

A Lady of Quality

THE *Corregidor*'s wife received her husband and his rustic escort in the main reception room of the residence.

She was standing there alone, her eyes fixed on the door.

She was a most noble lady, still quite young, of calm and severe beauty, more suited to the brush of a christian artist than the chisel of a pagan sculptor. She was dressed with all the nobility and gravity permitted by the style of the times. Her dress, with a short, narrow skirt, and short puffed sleeves, was made of black bombazine. A kerchief of white, slightly yellowing lace, covered her admirable shoulders and very long black tulle fingerless gloves swathed the greater part of her alabaster arms. She was cooling herself regally with an enormous fan, brought from the Philippine Islands.

With the other hand she held a lace handkerchief, whose four corners hung symmetrically, and with a balance only comparable with the rest of her demeanour and every little movement she made.

That beautiful woman resembled a queen and much more an abbess. Therefore she inspired respect and fear in all those who looked at her. Besides, the perfection of her dress at such a time of night, the gravity of her bearing and the many lights which illuminated the reception room showed that the *Corregidor*'s wife had taken extreme care to give that scene a theatrical solemnity and a formal tone which contrasted with the vulgarity and low nature of her husband's adventure.

Finally, it should he said that the lady was called Doña Mercedes Carrillo de Albornoz y Espinosa de los Monteros and that she was daughter, granddaughter, great-grand-daughter and twentieth granddaughter of the city, being a descendant of its illustrious conquerors. For reasons of worldly vanity, her family had obliged her to marry the old and wealthy *Corregidor*. Though she would have preferred to be a nun, for her natural inclinations led her towards the cloister, she consented to that painful sacrifice.

At the time of this story she already had two offspring from the dashing *Corregidor* from Madrid and it was still whispered that there were ships on the horizon again . . . but back to our story . . .

CHAPTER 31

An Eye for an Eye

'MERCEDES!' exclaimed the *Corregidor* as he came face to face with his wife. 'I have to know at once . . .'

'Hullo, Lucas! Fancy seeing you here!' interrupted the *Corregidor*'s wife. 'Is something wrong at the mill?'

'Señora! I'm in no mood for jokes!' answered the *Corregidor* in a furious rage. 'Before beginning my explanations, I must know what has happened to my good name . . .'

'That's nothing to do with me! Did you leave it in my care perhaps?'

'Yes, Señora, your care!' retorted Don Eugenio. 'Women are the guardians of their husbands' honour!'

'Well then, my dear Lucas, ask your wife . . . she's listening to us now.'

Señora Frasquita, who had stayed at the door of the room, uttered a sound like a roar.

'Come in, Señora, and sit down' added the *Corregidor*'s wife, turning to the miller's wife with the dignity of a queen. And she walked towards the sofa.

The generous Navarrese woman was able to understand immediately all the nobility of the attitude of the wronged and perhaps doubly wronged wife. So, rising at once to the same stature, she controlled her natural wish to burst out and kept a dignified silence. Of course, Frasquita was sure of her innocence and her strength and was in no hurry to defend herself. She certainly was in a hurry to accuse . . . a great hurry, but certainly not the *Corregidor*'s wife. She wanted to settle accounts with Lucas but Lucas was not there.

'Señora Frasquita,' repeated the noble lady seeing that the miller's wife had not moved from where she was standing. 'I told you to come in and sit down.'

This second invitation was made in a kinder and more sympathetic voice than the first. It was as if Doña Mercedes had also instinctively guessed, as she looked at the calm countenance and the severe beauty of the woman, that she was not dealing with a low person whom she could despise, but rather with another as unfortunate as she was herself.

Unfortunate, just for having met the *Corregidor*!

So, those two women who considered each other rivals twice over, exchanged glances of reconciliation and pardon, noting with great surprise that they were kindred souls, like two sisters who recognize each other after a long separation.

In the same way the chaste snows of lofty mountains perceive and greet each other from a distance.

Savouring these sweet emotions, the miller's wife swept into the room and sat down on the edge of a chair.

She had foreseen that she would have to pay some visits to important people in the city so, on her brief return to the mill she had tidied herself a little, and put on a black flannel mantilla, with large plush insets which set off her person divinely. She looked every inch a high-born lady.

As for the *Corregidor*, needless to say he had remained silent throughout that episode. Frasquita's roar of rage and hurt and her appearance on the scene must have shaken him. That woman now imbued him with more terror than his wife!

'So, Lucas,' went on Doña Mercedes, turning to her husband. 'There is Frasquita; you may ask her that question about your honour.'

'Mercedes, for the love of Christ!' shouted the *Corregidor*. 'You don't know how far I'll go. I tell you once more, stop joking and tell me everything that's happened here while I've been away! Where's that man?'

'Who? My husband? My husband's getting up and will be here soon.'

'Getting up?' brayed Don Eugenio.

'You're surprised? Where do you think a respectable man

ought to be at such a time of night except at home, in his bed, sleeping with his legitimate spouse as God commands?'

'Merceditas! Have a care what you say! See, they can all hear us! Remember I'm the *Corregidor*!'

'Don't you shout at me, Lucas, or I'll have the constables take you to prison,' retorted the *Corregidor*'s wife, and she stood up.

'Take me to prison! Me! The *Corregidor* of the city?'

'The *Corregidor* of the city, the representative of Justice, the delegate of the King,' replied the great lady with a sternness and vigour which stifled the voice of the feigned miller, 'reached home at the proper time, to rest from the noble tasks of his office, so that tomorrow he could continue to protect the honour and the lives of the citizens, the sanctity of the home and the modesty of women, preventing anyone from entering, disguised as a *Corregidor* or anything, else, the bedroom of somebody else's wife, so that nobody might overcome her virtue during her carefree rest, so that nobody could take advantage of her chaste sleep . . .'

'Merceditas! what are you suggesting?' whispered the *Corregidor* using only his lips and his gums. 'If that has really happened in my house then I say you are a hussy, a traitor and a whore!'

'Who is this man talking to?' Doña Mercedes broke in scornfully, casting her eyes over all the people standing round. 'Who is this madman? Who is this drunkard? I can't believe any longer that it's an honourable miller like Lucas even though he's wearing his peasant's clothes. Señor Juan López, believe me,' she went on, turning to face the village mayor who was terrified, 'my husband, the *Corregidor* of the city, reached his home two hours ago, with his three-cornered hat, his crimson cloak, his gentlemen's sword and his staff of office. The servants and constables who are here listening saw him walk through the porch and greeted him as he walked up the stairs and through the reception room. All the doors were closed at once and since then nobody has come in to my home except you. Is that true? Answer me, all of you!'

'It's true, absolutely true,' answered the nurse, the servants and the tipstaffs, all of whom were watching the astonishing scene from where they were standing in a bunch on the door-way.

'Get out of here, all of you!' screamed Don Eugenio, foaming at the mouth with rage. 'Garduña! Garduña! Come and arrest all these swine who are being disrespectful to me! To gaol, all of them. All of them to the gallows!'

Garduña was nowhere to be seen.

'Besides, Señor,' Doña Mercedes went on, changing her tone and now deigning to look at her husband and address him as such, in case the joke had gone too far. 'Let us assume you are my husband, let us suppose you are Don Eugenio de Zúñiga y Ponce de León . . . .'

'I am!'

'Let us also assume that I cannot be blamed for taking the man who came into my bedroom dressed as a *Corregidor* as you . . .'

'Miserable wretches!' shouted the old man, reaching for his sword and finding only its empty place, that is the miller's sash.

Frasquita covered her face with one side of her mantilla so as to hide the jealousy in her eyes.

'Let us assume anything you like,' went on Doña Mercedes with inexplicable impassivity. 'But, tell me, my good man, would you have any right to complain? Could you accuse me as the public prosecutor? Could you sentence me as a judge? Have you just been listening to a sermon? Have you just made confession? Have you just been to Mass? Where have you come from wearing those clothes? Where have you come from with that lady? Where have you spent half the night?'

'Please,' exclaimed Señora Frasquita, leaping up suddenly as if on a spring and crossing proudly between the *Corregidor*'s wife and her husband.

The latter was about to speak but stood there with his mouth open when he saw that she was going to enter the fray.

But Doña Mercedes forestalled her and said:

'Señora, don't exhaust yourself giving me explanations.

I'm not asking you for them, not in the least. Here comes somebody who can ask you for them as of right!'

At that moment, the door of a small side room opened and in the door appeared Lucas, dressed as the *Corregidor* from head to toe, and with staff, gloves and short sword as if he were about to present himself at the town council.

CHAPTER 32

Faith Can Move Mountains

'A VERY good evening to you,' declared Lucas, as he removed his three-cornered hat, speaking with his mouth pursed up like Don Eugenio de Zúñiga.

Then he walked into the room, swaying in every direction, and kissed the hand of the *Corregidor*'s wife.

Everybody was astounded. The similarity between Lucas and the *Corregidor* was astonishing, and so the servants and even Señor Juan López were unable to hold back a guffaw.

Don Eugenio was wounded by that fresh insult and hurled himself at Lucas like a basilisk.

But Señora Frasquita moved in and pushed the *Corregidor* away with the arm he knew of old. His Lordship, to avoid another tumble and the consequent ridicule, let himself be pushed around without a hint of protest. It was evident that the woman was destined to tame the poor old man.

Lucas grew pale as a ghost as he saw his wife approach, but he controlled himself at once and with a laugh so horrible that he had to place his hand over his heart to prevent it breaking into little pieces, he said, still imitating the *Corregidor*:

'God keep you, Frasquita. Have you sent your nephew his appointment yet?'

Frasquita was a sight to be seen then. She threw back her mantilla, looked up with the majesty of a lion and nailing two eyes like daggers into the false *Corregidor*.'

'I despise you, Lucas!' she said, straight to his face.

85

Everybody thought she had spat at him, such was her attitude, her mien and the tone of voice that emphasized her words.

The miller's face was transfigured, as he heard his wife's voice. A sort of inspiration, as of religious faith, had penetrated his mind, filling it with light and joy. So, forgetting for a moment everything he had seen or thought he had seen in the mill, he exclaimed with tears in his eyes and sincerity in his voice.

'So you are my Frasquita?'

'No!' she replied, beside herself with anger. 'I'm not your Frasquita any more! I am ... ask your deeds this night and they'll tell you what you've done with the heart that so loved you!'

And she burst into tears, like a mountain of ice which sinks and begins to melt.

Unable to restrain herself, Doña Mercedes rushed to her and held her most tenderly in her arms.

Frasquita began to kiss her, unaware of what she was doing, saying between her sobs, like a little girl seeking comfort from her mother.

'Señora, Señora, how unlucky I am!'

'Not as much as you think,' answered Doña Mercedes, also weeping copiously.

'I certainly am unfortunate,' groaned Lucas at the same time, dashing the tears from his eyes with his fists, as if ashamed of shedding them.

'Well, what about me?' Don Eugenio interrupted at length, feeling more tender because the weeping of the others affected him and hoping to save himself by the watery way, that is, by way of weeping. 'Oh, I'm no good, a monster, a bad one come to grief and I deserve all I get!'

And he burst into a miserable howl, embracing the portly middle of Señor Juan López.

And the latter and the servants were crying likewise and everything seemed to have concluded, yet nobody had explained their actions yet.

CHAPTER 33

Well, What about You?

LUCAS was the first to come to the surface in that sea of tears.

The reason was that he began to remember what he had seen through the keyhole.

'Now everybody, let's get things clear,' he said suddenly.

'There's nothing to be said, Lucas,' exclaimed Doña Mercedes. 'Your wife's a saint!'

'Of course ... yes ... but.'

'No buts! Let her speak and you'll see how she'll defend herself. When I saw her I knew in my heart she was a saint in spite of everything you had told me!'

'All right, let her speak!' said Lucas.

'I shan't speak,' answered the miller's wife. 'The one to speak is you! Because the truth is that you ...'

And Frasquita stopped then, unable to go on because of the great respect she felt for Doña Mercedes.

'Well, and what about you?' answered Lucas, losing all his trust again.

'We're not talking about her now,' cried the *Corregidor*, his jealousy burning again, 'we're talking about you and this lady ... oh! Merceditas! How could I ever dream that you ...'

'Well, what about you?' replied Doña Mercedes, looking him up and down.

And for some minutes the two couples repeated the same phrases over and over again.

'You.'

'Well what about you?'

'Fancy you!'

'And you!'

'But how could you?' Etc. etc. etc.

It would have gone on for ever if Doña Mercedes, robed once more in her dignity, had not said finally to Don Eugenio:

'Now you be quiet! We'll discuss our own affair privately later. The most important thing to do now is to reassure

87

Lucas. I think it would be very easy since I can see Señor Juan López and Toñuelo there both dying to excuse Señora Frasquita.'

'I don't need men to stand up for me,' replied Frasquita, 'I have two witnesses who are much more trustworthy and nobody can say I've seduced or suborned them!'

'And where are they?' asked the miller.

'Downstairs, at the door!'

'Well, tell them to come up, with my Lady's permission.'

'The poor girls wouldn't be able to come up.'

'Ah, it's two women then. There's trustworthy witnesses for you!'

'That's worse! It's probably two little girls. Kindly tell me their names.'

'One is called Piñona and the other Liviana.'

'Our two donkeys! Frasquita, you're laughing at me.'

'No, I'm being very serious. With the evidence of these two donkeys, I can prove to you that I wasn't in the mill when you saw the Señor *Corregidor* there.'

'For God's sake speak plainly.'

'Listen, Lucas, and I hope you die of shame for having doubted my virtue. While you were coming back tonight from the village to our home, I was on my way from our home to the village and so we passed on the road. But you weren't on the road or, rather, you had stopped to light some tinder in a field . . .'

'Yes, it's true I stopped . . . go on.'

'At that moment your donkey whinnied.'

'Exactly . . . oh, how happy I am! Go on, speak, speak, for every word of yours gives me back a year of my life!'

'And that whinny was answered by another one on the road.'

'Oh, yes, yes. God bless you! I can hear it now!'

'It was Liviana and Piñona who had recognized each other and were greeting each other like old friends, while we two didn't greet or even recognize each other.'

'Don't say any more! Don't say any more!'

'Not only did we not know each other,' went on Frasquita,

'but we both took fright and fled in opposite directions. So you can see that I wasn't in the mill! If you want to know why you found the Señor *Corregidor* in our bed, feel the clothes you are wearing which must still be damp and they'll tell you better than I can. His Lordship fell into the mill-race and Garduña took his clothes off and put him to bed! If you want to know why I opened the door, it was because I thought it was you who was drowning and crying out. And, lastly, if you want to know about my nephew's appointment . . . but that's all I have to say at the moment. When we're alone I'll tell you about that and lots of other things which I ought not to mention in front of this lady.'

'Everything that Señora Frasquita has said is gospel truth!' cried Señor Juan López, trying to ingratiate himself with Doña Mercedes, seeing that she ruled the roost in the *Corregidor*'s residence.

'Everything, everything,' added Toñuelo, following his master's line.

'So far, everything!' added the *Corregidor*, very pleased that Frasquita's explanations had stopped where they had.

'So, you're innocent!' exclaimed Lucas, admitting the evidence. 'My Frasquita, my darling Frasquita! Forgive the injustice I did you and let me kiss you!'

'That's another kettle of fish!' answered the miller's wife, slipping out of his grasp. 'Before I kiss you I must have an explanation from you.'

'I'll explain for him and for me,' said Doña Mercedes.

'I've been waiting for this for an hour,' said the *Corregidor*, trying to stand up straight.

'But I shan't do so,' continued his wife, turning her back in disdain on her husband, 'until these gentlemen have exchanged their clothes, and, even then, I'll give an explanation only to those who deserve to have one.'

'Come on then, let's change,' said the Murcian to Don Eugenio, happy that he had not murdered him but looking at him with real Moorish-style hate in his eyes. 'Your Lordship's clothes stifle me. I've been very unlucky all the time I had them on.'

'Because you are not fitted for them,' replied the *Corregidor*. 'But I, on the other hand, want to put them on so that I can hang you and half the world if the excuses of my wife do not satisfy me!'

When Doña Mercedes heard these words, she eased the company's mind with a gentle smile, like that of one of those patient angels whose task it is to watch over men.

CHAPTER 34

The Corregidor's *Wife is Pretty Also*

WHEN the *Corregidor* and Lucas had left the room, Doña Mercedes sat down again on the sofa. She placed Frasquita beside her and then said with friendly simplicity to the servants and tipstaffs who were crowding around the door:

'Come on then, boys! Now tell this excellent woman all the bad things you know about me!'

The Fourth Estate came forward and ten voices tried to speak at the same time but the wet-nurse, being the most important person below stairs, imposed silence and spoke in these words:

'You should know, Señora Frasquita, that My Lady and I were looking after the children this evening, waiting to see if the Master was coming and saying the Rosary for the third time to make the clock move faster. You see, Garduña had explained that the Señor *Corregidor* was hunting some very terrible criminals and we couldn't go to bed without seeing him come back safe. Then we heard people in the next door bedroom, which is where the master and mistress have their bed. We were frightened to death and took a light and went to see who was in the bedroom. Then, *Virgen del Carmen*! We went in and saw a man, dressed like the master, but it wasn't him (since it was your husband) trying to hide under the bed. "Thieves!" we began to shout at the tops of our voices and a moment later the room was full of people and the constables were dragging the false *Corregidor* from his hiding-place. My

Lady, like everyone else, had recognized Lucas. Seeing him wearing those clothes, she thought he had killed the master and began to weep so that it would have melted a stone: "To prison! To prison!" the rest of us were saying meanwhile. "Thief!" "Murderer!" were the best names that Lucas heard himself called, so he stood there like a dead man, against the wall, all meek and mild like. But when he saw they were going to take him to prison he said ... what I'm going to repeat, although it would be better not to:

' "Señora, I am neither a thief nor a murderer. The thief and the murderer of my honour is in my house, in bed with my wife." '

'Poor Lucas,' sighed Frasquita.

'Poor me,' said Doña Mercedes placidly.

'That's what we all said, "Poor Lucas and poor Señora". Because, to tell the truth, Señora Frasquita, we already had some idea that my master was attracted to you ... although nobody imagines that you ...'

'Nurse!' exclaimed Doña Mercedes severely. 'Stop there!'

'I'll tell the other part,' said a constable, taking advantage of the situation to get his word in. 'Lucas put it over us properly with his clothes and his style of walking when he came into the house, so much so that we really thought he was the Señor *Corregidor*. But he hadn't come with what we might call very good intentions and if the Señora hadn't been up, imagine what would have happened.'

'That's enough, you be quiet too!' interrupted the cook. 'That's a load of nonsense! Yes, Señora Frasquita, to explain what he was doing in my mistress's bedroom, he had to confess why he had come. Of course the Señora couldn't restrain herself when she heard him and gave him such a clout over his mouth that she knocked half his teeth down his throat! I also abused him and insulted him and tried to scratch his eyes out ... I mean, you know, Señora Frasquita, even if he is your husband ... him coming with evil intentions ...'

'You talk too much!' shouted the porter, standing in front of the orator. 'What would you expect him to have done? Now, Señora Frasquita, listen to me and let's get to the point.

The Señora did and said what she ought to . . . but later, when her anger cooled, she took pity on Lucas and began to think about the *Corregidor*'s bad actions and went as far as to say these or similar words:

' "However unworthy your intentions were, Lucas, and although I can never pardon such insolence, your wife and my husband should believe for a few hours that they've been hoist with their own petard and that, helped by your disguise, you've paid them back in their own coin. This is the best revenge we can have on them. It's deceit which is very easy to make good when it suits us."

'When they agreed to such an amusing plan of action, the Señora and Lucas gave us all a lesson on what we should say and do when His Lordship came back. And one thing's for sure. I gave Sebastián Garduña such a clout on his rump that I don't think he'll forget the night of Saint Simon and Saint Jude for a long time yet.'

Before the porter finished, the *Corregidor*'s wife and the miller's wife had been whispering into each other's ear for a long time, embracing and kissing all the time and occasionally unable to restrain their laughter.

What a pity that you couldn't hear what they were saying! But the reader will not have to make a great effort to imagine it, certainly not if she is a lady.

CHAPTER 35

The Royal Decree

JUST then the *Corregidor* and Lucas appeared again in the hall, this time in their own clothes.

'Now it's my turn,' said Don Eugenio as he swaggered in.

And after striking the floor with his staff a couple of times as if to recover his strength, just like an official Antaeus,* who had no strength till his malacca cane touched the ground,

---

* Son of Neptune and Earth, who derived strength from contact with earth. He was killed by Hercules.

he said to his wife with indescribably hypocritical pomposity:

'Mercedes, I await your explanation!'

Meanwhile the miller's wife had risen and given Lucas the pinch of peace. He gasped with relief and glanced at her, no longer angry and once more deeply in love. The *Corregidor* observed the pantomime and was taken back, unable to comprehend this unexplained reconciliation.

He addressed himself once more to his wife, each word dripping with venom:

'Señora. Everybody knows what his or her spouse has been up to except me . . . kindly enlighten me. I command you as your husband and the *Corregidor*.'

And he struck the floor once more.

'So you're going?' said Doña Mercedes, walking over to Señora Frasquita and ignoring Don Eugenio. 'Well, you needn't worry. None of this will have any repercussions. Rosa! Bring a light and show my guests out, they're going home. *Vaya con Dios*, Lucas.'

'Oh no!' shouted Zúñiga, putting himself between them and the door. 'Lucas isn't going anywhere. He's under arrest until I know everything that's happened. Constables! In the King's name!'

Not one servant obeyed Don Eugenio. They all looked to his wife for guidance.

'Come on man, let them pass,' she exclaimed, almost walking over her husband and saying good-bye to everybody courteously, with her head tilted to one side, lifting her skirt with the tips of her fingers and sinking gracefully until she completed the fashionable curtsey of the time called 'the peacock's tail'.

'But I . . . but you . . . but we . . . but they!' the old fool mumbled on, pulling his wife by her dress and upsetting her carefully begun curtsies.

It was all a waste of energy. Nobody took any notice of His Lordship!

When they had all gone and the ill-matched husband and wife were alone, Mercedes deigned at last to say to her husband in the tones that a Tzarina of all the Russias would use to inflict a sentence of exile for life in Siberia on an unsuccessful minister:

'You'll never know what happened in my bedroom tonight even if you live a thousand years. If you'd been in it, as you should have been, you wouldn't have had to ask anybody. As far as I'm concerned there's no longer any reason, and there never will be, for me to satisfy your curiosity, because I despise you so deeply that if you weren't the father of my children I'd throw you over that balcony right now, just as I'm throwing you out of my bedroom for good. So, good night, sir.'

These words having been pronounced, which Don Eugenio heard without blinking (he was very frightened when he was alone with his wife), Doña Mercedes went into the inner room and from there to her bedroom, shutting the doors behind her, and the poor man stood there in the middle of the room, muttering between clenched gums (as he had no teeth), with unmatched cynicism:

'Oh well, I've got off easier than I thought! Never mind, Garduña will find me another woman!'

CHAPTER 36

Conclusion, Moral and Epilogue

THE birds were chirping to greet the dawn when Lucas and Frasquita left the city on their way back to the mill.

The couple were walking and the two asses were plodding side by side ahead of them.

'On Sunday you'll have to go to Confession,' said the miller's wife to her husband, 'you've got to purify yourself from all the evil thoughts and plans you had last night!'

'Yes, that's a very good idea,' answered the miller, 'but at the same time you must do me a favour and that is to give the mattresses and linen on our bed to the poor and get new ones. I'll not sleep where that poisonous rat sweated!'

'Don't mention him to me, Lucas,' Frasquita flashed back.

'Let's talk about something else. I'd like to ask another favour . . .'

'Just ask with that sweet mouth . . .'

'Next summer take me to bathe at Solán de Cabras.'

'What for?'

'To see if we can have children.'

'Marvellous idea! I'll take you, if God wills.'

And then they reached the mill, just as the sun, which had not yet appeared, was already gilding the summits of the mountains.

In the afternoon, to the great surprise of the couple, who did not expect any more visits from important people after a scandal like that one, more gentry than ever came to the mill. The Venerable Prelate, many canons, the lawyer, two Priors and several other people (who, it was learnt later, had been summoned there by His Grace), literally filled the courtyard with the climbing vine.

Only the *Corregidor* was missing.

Once the assembly was gathered, the Bishop began to speak and said that, though certain things had happened in that house, his Canons and he himself would continue to go there as before, so that neither the honourable miller and his wife nor the other people there should be objects of public criticism, which was deserved only by the man who had profaned such a decent and respectable gathering with his ignoble conduct. He exhorted Frasquita paternally to be less provocative and tempting in the future in her speech and demeanour and to try and keep her arms more covered and the neckline of her dress higher. He advised Lucas not to be so eager for profit, to be more circumspect and not so forward in his attitude to his betters. He finished by giving his blessing to all and saying that, as he was not fasting that day, he would have great pleasure in eating a couple of bunches of grapes.

And that was the opinion of all . . . as far as this last was concerned, and the climbing vine was not allowed to rest that afternoon! The miller calculated that it cost him two *arrobas**
of grapes.

* About 50 lb.

These pleasant gatherings went on for nearly three years, until, contrary to everybody's forecast, the armies of Napoleon invaded the peninsula and the Peninsular War began.

My Lord Bishop, the Prebendary and the Canon-Confessor died in 1808, the lawyer and the other people who used to come, in the years 1809, 1810, 1811 and 1812, unable to bear the sight of the French, Poles and other vermin who invaded the country and smoked their pipes in the chancels of the churches, during church parades!

The *Corregidor*, who never went back to the mill, was dismissed by a French marshal and died in a prison in Madrid, not having wanted for a single minute – to his great credit – to come to an agreement with the enemy ruler.

Doña Mercedes, who did not remarry, brought her children up with extreme care, and when she was old, retired to a convent where she ended her days considered by all a saint.

Garduña became an ally of the French.

Señor Juan López was a guerrilla and commanded a band, but was killed, with his constable, in the famous battle of Baza, not without killing a large number of Frenchmen.

Finally, Lucas and Frasquita, though they never had children in spite of visiting Solán de Cabras and making many vows and supplications, still went on loving each other in the same way, and reached a great age. They saw Absolutism disappear in 1812 and 1820, and reappear in 1814 and 1823 until finally the constitutional system was really introduced on the death of the Absolute King, Ferdinand VII. Then they went on to a better life, precisely as the first Carlist War broke out in 1833. And the top hats that everybody was now wearing could not make them forget 'those times' symbolized by the three-cornered hat.

CAPTAIN POISON

CHAPTER I

A Little Political History

ON the afternoon of 26 March 1848, there was an exchange of shots and knife thrusts in Madrid between a handful of civilians who uttered, as they died, the until then foreign cry of *Viva la República!*, and the army of the Spanish monarchy, (a force introduced by Ataulf, the Visigoth King, reconstituted by Don Pelayo and reformed by Trastamara), whose commander, in the name of Queen Isabel II, was, at the time, the Prime Minister and Minister of War, Don Ramón María Narváez . . .

And that is enough of history and politics, Let us pass on to less well-known but more pleasant matters, which had their origin in those melancholy events.

CHAPTER 2

Our Heroine

IN the left-hand flat on the ground floor of a humble but elegant and clean house in the Calle de Preciados, a very narrow, twisting street in those days and centre of the disturbance of that moment, there lived alone, that is, without the company of any man, three good, compassionate women who differed greatly in appearance and social status, in that one was an older lady, a widow, a native of the province of Guipúzcoa, of grave and noble appearance. The second, her daughter, young, single, a native of Madrid and quite pretty, though very different from her mother (which meant that she took after her father in everything) and, finally, a servant,

97

impossible to qualify or describe, of indeterminate age, appearance and almost of sex, baptized, up to a point, in Mondoñedo and to whom we have already been over-generous (as was in fact that priest) by recognizing that in fact she belonged to the human race.

The younger lady seemed the symbol or personification, in skirts, of common sense; such was the balance between her beauty and her naturalness, her elegance and her simplicity, her wit and her modesty. It was easy for her to walk unnoticed along a street, without exciting the attentions of the professional gallant, yet it was impossible for anyone to fail to admire her and be struck by her many charms as soon as he looked at her attentively. She was not (or rather, she had no wish to be) one of those showy, elaborate and overwhelming beauties who attract all eyes the moment they enter a drawing-room or theatre, or promenade along the street, and who embarrass or cast the poor devil accompanying them into the shade, be he their husband, fiancé, father, or Prester John himself ... hers was a wise and harmonious concert of physical and moral perfection. Her astonishing excellence did not thrill at first, just as peace or good order are not at once evident. She was like a well-proportioned monument where nothing strikes the observer and makes him marvel until he comes to the conclusion that, if everything looks smooth, easy and natural, it is because everything is beautiful. One would say that this honoured goddess of the middle class had studied her style of dressing, arranging her hair, looking, moving, in other words of handling the treasures of her splendid youth in such a way that nobody would consider her vain, presumptuous or provocative, but very different from those deities in the marriage market who display their charms and walk up and down announcing to all and sundry: 'This house is for sale ... or rent.'

But let us not dally with flowery language or descriptions, for there is much to tell and very little time at our disposal.

CHAPTER 3

Our Hero

THE Republicans were firing at the troops from the corner of the Calle de Peregrinos and the troops were shooting at the Republicans from the Puerta de Sol, so that bullets from both sides passed in front of the windows of the ground floor flat and even struck the iron bars in front of the windows, making them vibrate stridently, ricocheting into the venetian blinds, wooden shutters and glass panes.

The mother . . . and the maid were both very afraid, though the nature of their fears and their way of expressing them were dissimilar. The noble widow feared first for her daughter, then for the rest of mankind and finally for herself; the Galician woman feared more than anything for her own skin, and secondly for her stomach and that of her mistresses, for the water jar was nearly empty and the baker had not appeared with the afternoon bread. In the last place she feared just a little for any soldiers or civilians from Galicia who might be killed or lose something in the conflict. We shall not speak of the fears of the daughter because either they were neutralized by her curiosity or because there was no place for them in her nature, more manly than female. In fact, the gently nurtured maiden, deaf to the advice and orders of her mother and the laments and howls of the maid, both of whom were hiding in the interior rooms, slipped out from time to time to the rooms which looked on to the street and even opened the wooden shutters of a window so that she could form an exact opinion of the nature and progress of the struggle.

During one of these highly dangerous excursions, she saw that the troops had advanced as far as the door of the house, while the rebels were retreating to the Plaza de Santo Domingo, not without continuing to fire in alternate ranks with admirable calm and courage. And she also saw that at the head of the soldiers and even of the officers, one man was outstanding in his energetic and intrepid demeanour and the fiery phrases with which he harangued them all. He was about forty, distinguished and elegant in bearing and of delicate, handsome though hard expression, as thin and strong as a bunch of muscles, tallish in stature and clad partly in civilian dress and partly in uniform. That is to say, he wore a forage cap with the three small chevrons of a captain, a civilian frock coat and trousers of black cloth, an Infantry officer's sabre and the bandolier and musket of a *chasseur* (of rabbits and partridges, that is). It was precisely this amazing person that the young girl was watching and admiring, when the Republicans fired a volley at him, doubtless considering that he was more to be feared than the others, or because they supposed he was a general, cabinet minister or something of the sort.

The poor Captain, or whatever he was, fell to the ground as if struck by lightning, with his face covered in blood, while the rebels fled happily, very satisfied with their deed, with the soldiers in pursuit, eager to avenge their unfortunate chief.

So the street emptied and fell silent and in the middle of it, stretched out and bleeding heavily, lay that valiant gentleman, who had perhaps not died yet and whom it was just possible that kind and merciful hands could preserve from the clutches of death. The young woman did not hesitate for a moment. She ran to her mother and the servant, explained the situation and told them there was no more firing in the Calle de Preciados. She had to do battle, not so much with the prudent vacillation of the generous Guipuzcoan lady, as with the purely animal terror of the shapeless Galician, and in a few minutes the three women were bodily carrying into their honourable house and placing on the luxurious bed of the widow, in the bedroom of honour off the main room, the unconscious body of the man who, though not the real protagonist of the events of the twenty-sixth of March, is the main personage of this particular story.

CHAPTER 4

One's Own Skin and Other People's

THE charitable ladies soon realized that the gallant Captain was not dead, but merely unconscious as a result of a bullet which had struck him a glancing blow on the forehead, yet had merely grazed the skin. They also saw that he had a bullet through his right leg, which was perhaps fractured, and that the wound should not be left for a single moment, as it was bleeding copiously. That is to say, they were soon aware that the only useful and practical thing to do for the unfortunate gentleman was to call a doctor without delay . . .

'Mama,' said the brave young woman, 'Doctor Sánchez lives just a few yards from here, on the other side of the street . . . I think Rosa should go and fetch him. It won't take a minute and she won't be in any danger.'

At that moment a shot was fired very close, followed by three or four more fired consecutively and from farther away. Then absolute silence reigned again.

'I shan't go!' grumbled the maid. 'Those were shots, just now. I'm sure miss and madam wouldn't want me to be shot in the middle of the street.'

'Stupid girl! There's nothing in the street!' retorted the young woman, who had just looked out of one of the barred windows.

'Get away from there, Angustias!' shouted her mother when she saw what she was doing.

'The first shot,' Angustias went on, 'which was answered by the troops from the Puerta de Sol, must have come from the attic of number 19. It must have been fired by a very ugly man whom I can see reloading his musket . . . so, the bullets are flying very high and it's not in the least dangerous to cross our street. But, on the other hand, it would be a most shameful thing to allow that poor man to die just to save ourselves a little trouble!'

'I'll go and get the doctor,' said the mother, who had just finished bandaging the Captain's leg as best she could.

'Oh no!' cried the daughter, darting into the bedroom. 'What would people say about me? I'll go. I'm younger and I can walk faster. You've suffered enough already in your life from these awful wars!'

'All the same, you're not going,' repeated her mother imperiously.

'Nor am I!' added the maid.

'Mama, let me go. I beg of you on my father's memory! I haven't the heart to see that brave man die from loss of blood when we can save him. Look! Look how little use your bandages are. The blood's already seeping through the mattress.'

'Angustias! I've told you you're not to go!'

'I shan't go, if you don't want me to. But Mother, just think that if my father, your noble and courageous husband, had not died as he did, from loss of blood in the middle of the wood the night after a battle, if some charitable hand had staunched the blood from his wounds . . .'

'Angustias!'

'Mama! Let me go! I'm as Aragonese and as stubborn as my father, even though I was born in this good-for-nothing Madrid. In any case, I don't believe women have been granted any dispensation from having as much self-respect and valour as men.'

Those were the words of that fine girl. Her mother had not got over her astonishment, mixed with a certain respect or admiration in spite of herself at this magnificent outburst, when Angustias was already fearlessly crossing the Calle de Preciados.

CHAPTER 5

The Musket Shot

'LOOK at her, madam! Just look how fine she goes!' cried the Galician servant, clapping her hands and watching our heroine from the window . . .

But alas! that very moment, a shot was fired, very close by, and when the poor old widow, who was also at the window, saw her daughter stop and touch her clothes, she uttered a piercing scream and fell on her knees almost unconscious.

'She's not hit! She's not hit!' the servant was shouting. 'She's already going into the house opposite. It's all right, madam!'

But the widow could not hear her. As pale as a ghost, she fought her depression until she found strength in her very distress and, getting up, ran half-mad into the street ... in the middle of which she found her intrepid daughter Angustias already returning followed by the doctor.

Mother and daughter embraced and kissed with uncontrolled joy, standing exactly over the stream of blood shed by the Captain. Finally they went into the house without anybody noticing that there was a hole in the young woman's skirts caused by the treacherous musket shot fired by the man in the attic when he saw her crossing the street.

It was the Galician servant who not only noticed the hole but was unfeeling enough to announce her discovery.

'Them's hit 'er. Them's hit 'er!' she cried in the grammar of Mondoñedo. 'I were right not to go out. Big 'oles them 'ud made in my three flannel petticoats!'

We may imagine how the mother's fears were renewed, until Angustias convinced her she was unharmed. And all there remains to say is that, as we shall see, the poor Guipuzcoan lady would not enjoy a moment of good health from that frightful day onward.

And now let us look at the unfortunate Captain and see what opinion of his injuries was formed by the diligent and expert Doctor Sánchez.

CHAPTER 6

Diagnosis and Prognosis

THE doctor enjoyed an enviable reputation, justified by the swift and effective emergency treatment that he gave to our hero, using household remedies to staunch the blood which flowed from his wounds, and setting and splinting his fractured leg, helped only by the three women. But the good gentleman did not explain his knowledge with the same efficiency, for he suffered from the oratorical vice of stating the obvious.

Certainly he would guarantee the Captain's life, 'assuming he would come out of that deep coma in twenty-four hours', a sign of profound cerebral commotion caused by the wound which he had suffered from an oblique projectile (discharged from a fire-arm without breaking, though bruising, the frontal bone) 'precisely where he had the wound, as a result of this unfortunate civil strife and his having involved himself with it'. He added at once by way of commentary, that, as to whether the above-mentioned cerebral commotion would indeed cease within the twenty-four hours, he would reserve his prognosis until the next evening.

He repeated these self-evident statements at length and then recommended several times and somewhat tiresomely (being doubtless familiar with the daughters of Eve), that when the patient recovered consciousness they should not allow him to speak and they should not speak about anything to him, however urgent it might seem to them. He left verbal instructions and written prescriptions for all situations and circumstances that might occur and arranged to come the next day, even if fighting was still going on, since he was as consummate a man as he was a good doctor and harmless orator. Off he went home, just in case another similar urgency demanded his attention, not however, without advising the disturbed widow to go to bed early, as her pulse was irregular and she might very well have a small temperature by the time night fell (which it had already done).

CHAPTER 7

Expectation

IT must have been about three o'clock in the morning. Though she was actually rather ill, the noble lady was still at her sick guest's bedside, paying scant heed to the pleading of her tireless daughter Angustias, who had not only remained awake, but had not even yet sat down that night.

The young woman stood at the foot of the blood-soaked bed as thin and motionless as a statue, not taking her eyes from the white face, like an ivory Christ, of the valiant warrior whom she had so greatly admired in the afternoon. So she waited, with evident anxiety, for the luckless man to awake from his profound coma which could well end in death.

If anyone snored it was the wretched Galician servant in the best armchair in the room, with her empty head slumped on her knees. She had not even realized that the armchair possessed a back, which was very suitable for resting the occiput.

In the course of the long vigil, mother and daughter had exchanged several opinions and hazarded conjectures on the Captain's social status, his character, his ideas and his feelings. With the minuteness of observation that women preserve even in the most terrible and solemn circumstances they had remarked on the fine quality of his shirt, his handsome watch, his scrupulous cleanliness and the marquess's crowns embroidered on his socks. Nor did they fail to notice a very old, gold medallion which he wore around his neck under his clothes, nor that the medallion bore an image of the Virgin of the Pillar of Zaragoza; all these observations made them extremely happy, for they led them to conclude that the Captain was a gentleman, of good Christian upbringing. Naturally they respected the contents of his pockets, where there might perhaps have been letters or cards which bore his name and address. This was information which they hoped that he himself, with God's help, could give them when he recovered consciousness and the power of speech, indicating that he was not going to die . . .

Though the disturbances had stopped for the time being with the Monarchy victorious in the conflict, from time to time some distant and unanswered shot was heard as if it were a solitary protest by some Republican or other not converted by grapeshot, and the echoing trot of cavalry patrols riding around keeping order in the streets; both sounds were dismal and ominous, and very sad to hear from the bedside of a wounded and almost dead soldier.

CHAPTER 8

Difficulties in the Visitor's Guide

THAT was the situation when, shortly after the clock in the Church of the Buen Suceso had chimed half past three, the Captain suddenly opened his eyes, glanced angrily round the room, stared first at Angustias and then at her mother, with a sort of a childish terror, and stammered nervously:

'Where the devil am I?'

The young woman put her fingers to her lips, advising him not to speak, but the widow had been very offended by the third word in the Captain's question and hastened to reply:

'You are in a decent, safe place. This is my house and I am the widow of General Barbastro, Count of Santurce, at your service.'

'Women! What the hell!' stammered the Captain, closing his eyes as if relapsing into his coma.

But it was very soon obvious that he was breathing easily and strongly, indicating that he was sleeping peacefully.

'He's going to live!' said Angustias very calmly. 'Father will be pleased with us.'

'I was praying for his soul,' answered her mother, 'though you can see that our patient's first greeting left much to be desired.'

'I know,' uttered the Captain slowly, his eyes still closed, 'the General Staff Army List, printed in the *Visitor's Guide*, by heart. There isn't and there hasn't been, in this century, any General Barbastro in it!'

'Let me explain!' exclaimed the widow excitedly. 'My late husband . . .'

'Don't answer him now, Mama,' interrupted the young woman with a smile, 'he's wandering and we must be careful with his poor head. Remember Doctor Sánchez's instructions!'

The Captain opened his handsome eyes, fixed his glance on Angustias and closed them again, saying more slowly still:

'I never wander, madam! In fact I always tell the truth to everyone, whatever the consequences!'

And having said this, syllable by syllable, he sighed deeply as if he were very tired after having spoken so long, and began to snore deeply, as if in his death agony.

'Are you asleep, Captain?' asked the widow in great alarm.

The wounded man did not reply.

CHAPTER 9

More Difficulties in the Visitor's Guide

'LET's allow him to rest,' said Angustias quietly as she sat down next to her mother, 'and since he can't hear us now, please allow me to tell you something, Mama. I don't think it was a good idea to tell him that you were a countess and a general's widow.'

'Why not?'

'Because . . . you know very well, we don't have the where-withal to care for or look after someone like him in the way *real* countesses or generals' widows would.'

'What do you mean, "real"?' exclaimed the widow excited-ly. 'Are you also questioning my rank? I'm just as much a countess as the Countess of Montijo and my husband was a general as much as Espartero!'

'Yes, of course you are, but until the Government makes up its mind about your application for a widow's pension, we'll be very poor.'

'Not as poor as all that! I've still got a thousand *reales* left from the emerald earrings and I have a pearl choker with a diamond clasp. My grandfather gave me it and it's worth more than five hundred *duros*. That's more than enough for us to live on until my case is settled, which won't take a month, and to look after this man as we should, even if he has to stay here two or three months because of his broken leg . . . you know the Clerk of the Council thinks I come under Article 10 of the Vergara agreement because, even though your father died before, we can prove he agreed with Maroto. . . .'*

'Santurce, Santurce. That county's not in the *Visitor's Guide* either . . .' muttered the Captain indistinctly, without opening his eyes.

Then, shaking off his weariness and almost sitting up in bed, he said, in a powerful, vibrant voice, as if he were already cured:

'Let's clarify this, madam. I must know where I am and who you are. Nobody orders me about or tricks me! God, this leg hurts.'

'Captain, you insult us!' exclaimed the General's widow, losing her temper.

'Now Captain, be quiet and stop talking,' said Angustias at the same time, in a calm voice, although she was also annoyed. 'Your life will be greatly endangered if you don't keep silent or don't lie still. Your right leg is broken and you have a wound in your head which has kept you unconscious for more than ten hours . . .'

'That's true!' exclaimed the strange man, putting his hands to his head and feeling the bandages that the doctor had put

* Maroto was leader of the moderate wing of the Carlist faction. In 1839 he met the Prime Minister and General, Espartero, and concluded the Peace of Vergara, permitting the defeated Carlists to retain their military ranks and titles of nobility.

on it. 'That mob wounded me! But who had the temerity to bring me into a strange house, when I have my own and there are civil and military hospitals? I don't like putting anybody to trouble, nor owing favours, which damn me if I deserve or want to deserve! I was in the Calle de Preciados . . .'

'And that's where you are now, number 14, ground floor . . .' interrupted the widow, ignoring her daughter, who was trying to signal her not to answer. 'We don't need to be thanked for anything by you because we haven't and we won't do anything more than what God commands and christian charity requires. Furthermore, you are in a respectable house. I am Doña Teresa Carrillo de Albornoz y Azpeitia, widow of the Carlist General Don Luis Gonzaga de Barbastro, agreed at *Vergara* (do you understand? *Agreed at Vergara*, though it was *posthumous, retrospective and implicit*, as it says in my applications). He owed his title of Count of Santurce to a Royal warrant of Carlos V, that Doña Isabel II must confirm, according to Article 10 of the Vergara agreement. I never tell lies, nor use false names, nor intend to do anything else with you than look after you and save your life, since Providence has entrusted me with the task.'

'Mama, don't excite him,' remarked Angustias. 'Can't you see that he's not calming down but getting ready to answer you even more fiercely? The poor man is ill and a little weak in the head. Captain! Be quiet and think about staying alive.'

The noble maiden spoke in her usual serious tone. But this did not tranquillize the Captain. He stared at her enraged, like a cornered wild boar attacked by a new and more fearsome enemy and exclaimed bravely:

CHAPTER 10

The Captain Defends Himself

'YOUNG lady! In the first place I'm not weak in the head nor have I ever been, and the proof of it is that no bullet has ever been able to penetrate it. In the second place, I'm extremely sorry to hear you speak about me with such pity and gentleness, because I'm not a person for gentle speech, soft soap or namby-pambiness. I'm sorry if I speak bluntly but we're all as God made us and I don't like anybody to get the wrong idea about me. I don't know what it is about me but I'd rather people shot at me than treated me kindly! So, let me warn you not to treat me gently because you'll make me burst, right here in this bed where I'm kept because of my bad luck ... I wasn't born to receive favours, or thank or pay people for them, so I've always tried to have nothing to do with women, children, or religious humbugs, or any other gentle or sweet people ... I'm a terrible man, whom nobody has ever been able to tolerate, as a boy, youth or old man, which is what I'm beginning to be ... all over Madrid I'm called Captain Poison! So you can go to bed and as soon as day comes, you can arrange for me to be taken to the General Hospital on a stretcher! There you are!'

'Mercy! What a man!' exclaimed Doña Teresa with horror.

'They should all be like me!' answered the Captain. 'The world would be a better place, or else it would have stopped a long time ago.'

Angustias smiled again.

'Don't smile, young lady. You're just mocking a poor sick man who can't run away and has to look at you,' the wounded man went on, with a hint of melancholy in his voice. 'Oh, I know only too well what an unmannerly boor I must seem to you. Believe me, I'm very sorry. But, on the other hand, I'd hate you to think I was deserving of your respect and then for you to find you'd made a mistake. Oh! If I could find the wretch who brought me here, just to annoy you and dishonour me ...'

'It was me, the young miss and madam. We carried you in,' said the Galician servant, who had been awakened by the shouting of the enraged Captain. 'You were bleeding to death outside the door of the house, sir, and then the young miss was sorry for you. I was also sorry – a bit. And as madam was sorry as well, we brought you in between the three of us. You don't half weigh a ton and you such a thin one an' all!'

The Captain's hackles rose when he saw yet another woman appear, but the story the Galician told him made such an impression that he could not stop himself saying:

'It's a pity you did not do that good deed for a better man than me. Why did you have to meet the incorrigible Captain Poison?'

Doña Teresa glanced at her daughter, as if to imply that the man was much less evil and ferocious than he thought he was. Her eyes met those of Angustias, who was still smiling with exquisite charm, meaning that she was of the same opinion. Meanwhile, the mournful Galician was saying tearfully:

'Well, you'd be even sorrier if you knew that the young miss went by herself to fetch the doctor to dress your two bullet wounds and, when the poor girl was in the middle of the road, they fired a shot at her and look! There's a hole in her overskirt!'

'And I should never have told you, Captain, for fear of irritating you,' explained the young woman, with a sort of mocking charm, lowering her eyes and smiling even more enchantingly than before. 'But since Rosa must tell everything, the only thing I can do is beg you to pardon me for the fright I caused my poor mother, as a result of which she still has a temperature.'

The Captain was astonished, his mouth wide open, looking in turn at Angustias, Doña Teresa and the maid. When the young woman had finished, he closed his eyes, uttered what sounded like a sort of roar, and exclaimed, with both fists clenched and pointing heavenwards:

'You're cruel! You're turning the knife in my wound. So, then, the three of you think you're going to make me your slave and the butt of your wit, do you? So, you think you are going to make me weep and talk soft, do you? So, I'm lost if I can't escape, am I? Right. I'll escape. That's all I needed! After all these years to end up as the plaything of three nice ladies. Madam!' he went on with great emphasis, addressing himself to the widow. 'If you don't go to bed straight away and drink a cup of lime tea with orange-blossom in it after you're in bed, I'll tear off these bandages and rags, and I'll die in five minutes, even if God doesn't want me to! As for you, Señorita Angustias, kindly call the night watchman and tell him to go to the house of the Marquess of Los Tomillares, Carrera de San Francisco, number— and inform him that his cousin Jorge de Córdoba is waiting for him here, seriously wounded. Then you will go to bed at once and leave me in the care of this intolerable Galician woman, who will from time to time give me some sugared water, the only thing I'll need until my cousin Alvaro comes. That's all, Countess. You go to bed first!'

Mother and daughter winked at each other. The former answered tranquilly:

'I shall give you an example of obedience and good sense. Good night, Captain. Sleep well.'

'I want to be obedient as well,' added Angustias, after making a note of the real name of Captain Poison and his cousin's address, 'but I am very sleepy, please allow me to put off sending the message to the Marquess de Los Tomillares until tomorrow. Good night. Don Jorge, be careful not to move!'

'I'm not staying alone with this gentleman!' shouted the Galician. 'He's got the devil of a temper and he makes my hair stand on end. He makes me tremble like a leaf!'

'Don't worry, beautiful . . .' answered the captain, 'I'll be gentler and more friendly with you than with your mistress.'

Doña Teresa and Angustias could not help laughing outright at this first sally of good humour from their intolerable guest.

And that is how, by fate and chance, such sad and tragic scenes as those of that afternoon and night were crowned by a little joy and happiness. It is so true that in this world everything is fleeting and transitory, both happiness and pain. In other words, time heals all things.

CHAPTER 11

The Doctor Comes Again

NEXT morning, by the mercy of God, there was no longer any sign of barricades or riots, a mercy which would last until 7 May that same year when the terrible scenes of the Plaza Mayor occurred. At eight o'clock that morning, Dr Sánchez was at the self-styled Countess of Santurce's house putting a permanent dressing and splint on Captain Poison's broken leg.

The Captain had taken it into his head that morning to remain silent. Before the painful dressing began, he had opened his lips only once, to make two brief and sharp observations to Doña Teresa and Angustias in answer to their friendly 'good morning'.

To the mother he said:

'For Christ's sake, Señora, why have you got up if you're ill? Just to make me more annoyed and ashamed, I suppose. Are you thinking of killing me with your attentions?'

And to Angustias he said:

'What does it matter if I'm worse or better? Be frank now! Have you sent for my cousin to take me out of here so that there's an end to interference and fussing?'

'Yes, Captain Poison! The porter's wife took the message half an hour ago,' answered the young woman very calmly as she straightened the pillows.

As for the easily angered Countess, of course she had bridled again at hearing a further spate of rudeness from her guest and so, she resolved not to speak to him again and limited herself to making lime tea and bandages, asking the impassive Dr Sánchez now and then, with lively interest, how the patient was (without deigning to give him a name) and if he would walk with a limp and whether he could have some chicken soup and ham at midday and if they should put sand down in the road so that the traffic noise should not trouble him, etc.

With his usual simplicity, the doctor assured them that

there was nothing to fear from the bullet wound to the head, thanks to the energetic and healthy constitution of the patient, who no longer had any symptoms of concussion or brain fever, but his diagnosis with regard to the fractured leg was not so favourable. Again he described it as serious and very dangerous, since the tibia was shattered, and he insisted that Don Jorge should remain absolutely still if he wanted to escape amputation or even death.

The doctor spoke calling a spade a spade, not only because he lacked the cunning to disguise his thoughts, but because he had already formed a very clear image of the obstinate and turbulent character of the man, who resembled a spoilt child. But, even that did not manage to scare the Captain, rather it drew a smile of disbelief and scorn from him.

It was the three women who caught a fright: Doña Teresa, out of simple kindness, Angustias, because of a certain noble determination and pride that she now had in healing and taming that heroic and peculiar man, and the maid, out of instinctive terror for anything which signified blood, mutilation, and death.

The Captain noticed the fright of his nurses and, though he had endured Dr Sánchez's ministrations with calm, he now said to him angrily:

'I say! You might have kept your remarks for my ears! Being a good doctor doesn't excuse you from having some thought for others' feelings. You can see what miserable faces you've given my three Marias.'

There the patient had to stop, overcome by the terrible pain caused by the doctor setting the fracture.

'Bah!' he went on afterwards. 'Fancy me staying on here! There's nothing I hate more than seeing women cry.'

The poor Captain was silent again and bit his lips for a few moments, though without uttering even a sigh. Clearly the pain was very great.

'Besides, Señora,' he said, addressing himself to Doña Teresa, 'I don't think you've any cause to look at me like that as if you hated me, because my cousin Alvaro can't be long in coming now and then you'll all be free of Captain

Poison! Then this worthy doctor (God man, don't press so hard) will see how well four soldiers will take me home on a stretcher and put an end to all their nonsense ... and they won't bother about moving my leg either (strewth, you're heavy-handed!). You'd think it was a nunnery! That's all I need. Broth, for me! Chicken essence, for me! Put sand down in the street, for me! What am I? Some sort of cardboard soldier to be fussed about and kept in a cotton wool box?'

Doña Teresa, impelled by the aggressiveness which was her only weakness and clearly not noticing how much pain Jorge was going through, was about to reply when, happily, there was a knock at the door and Rosa announced the Marquess of Tomillares.

'Thank God!' they all exclaimed at the same time, though in different tones and with different meanings.

The Marquess had come just as the doctor was finishing his treatment.

Jorge was sweating with pain. Angustias gave him a little vinegar and water and the patient breathed happily and said:

'Thanks, treasure.'

At that moment, the Marquess, led by the General's widow, entered the sick room.

CHAPTER 12

The Rainbow of Peace

DON Alvaro de Córdoba y Alvarez de Toledo was a man of most distinguished appearance, completely clean-shaven, and shaven already at that time of the morning. He was about sixty years old, with a round, mild and friendly face which revealed his placid and benign nature. So neat, symmetrical and perfect was his attire that he seemed the very personification of method and order.

And, considering that he was concerned and agitated about his relative's accident, he did not reveal even the slightest lack of self-control or fail in the least to comply with the canons of the most exquisite courtesy. He greeted Angustias and the doctor politely and even the Galician, though the Señora de Barbastro had not introduced her. Only then did he fix his eyes on the Captain. His glance was long, like that of a severe yet loving father, who accepts the prodigal and consoles his misfortunes, and admits the consequences though not the causes of yet another escapade.

Meanwhile Doña Teresa and especially Rosa, who did not stop talking (and made a point of referring to her mistress several times by both her titles, still *sub judice*) informed the courtly Marquess, without his asking, of everything that had happened in and around the house since the first shot had rung out the previous afternoon, not forgetting Don Jorge's unwillingness to allow himself to be cared for and taken pity on by the women who had saved his life.

As soon as the General's widow and the Galician had stopped talking, the Marquess questioned Doctor Sánchez, who told him about the Captain's wounds in a way with which we are already familiar, insisting that he should not be moved at all, at the risk of imperilling his recovery and even his life.

Finally, the worthy Don Alvaro turned towards Angustias as if to question her or inquire if she wished to add anything to what had been said by the others. Seeing that the young woman was content to shake her head, His Excellency prepared his nasal and laryngeal cavities to speak and adopted the alert and grave bearing of a man about to orate in the Senate (he was a senator) and said in a tone both serious and affable ... (But this speech should go in a paragraph by itself, in case at any time it is ever included in the *Complete Works* of the Marquess, who was also a literary man ... one of those described as 'respectable'.)

CHAPTER 13

The Power of Eloquence

'LADIES and gentleman, in the midst of our affliction and, dispensing with political considerations regarding the events which occurred yesterday, it seems to me that we cannot in any way complain . . .'

'No, of course you can't! There's nothing wrong with you. But when will I have a turn to speak?' interrupted Captain Poison.

'You won't, my dear Jorge,' replied the Marquess gently. 'I know you far too well to need you to explain your positive or negative acts to me. All I need to know is what these good people have told me.'

It was already noticeable that, either through profound respect or scorn, the Captain systematically avoided contradicting his illustrious cousin. He crossed his arms resignedly, stared at the ceiling of the bedroom and began to whistle the revolutionary *Himno de Riego*.

'I was saying,' went on the Marquess, 'that the best thing possible has come out of this tragedy. This new misfortune that has been brought on himself by my incorrigible and most dear cousin Don Jorge de Córdoba, whom nobody ordered to throw his hat into the ring during our little disturbance yesterday (for he is awaiting posting as usual and he ought to have learnt by now not to imitate heroes of adventure stories), is easily remedied, or was, happily, at the opportune moment, thanks to the heroism of this gallant young lady, to the charitable sentiments of the widow of the late General Barbastro, Countess of Santurce, to the skill of our worthy Doctor in Medicine and Surgery Señor Sánchez, whose fame has been known to me for several years, and to the zeal of this diligent servant . . .'

Here the Galician began to weep.

'Now let us move on to the positive side,' went on the

Marquess, who, it seemed, had a special gift for classifications and boundaries and thus would have made an excellent agricultural expert. 'Ladies and gentlemen, since, in the opinion of science and with the consent of common sense, it would be most perilous to move our most interesting patient and cousin Don Jorge de Córdoba from this hospitable bed, I resign myself to his disturbing this tranquil dwelling until he can be moved to mine or to his. But let it be understood, my dear cousin, that all this is assuming that your generous nature and the illustrous name you bear will lead you to dispense with certain nasty habits more suitable to the school, barracks or club, and avoid upsetting or troubling the worthy lady and her noble daughter, who efficiently seconded by their energetic and robust servant, preserved you from dying in the middle of the street . . . Don't answer back! You know I think things out very carefully before making arrangements and I never go back on my decisions. Furthermore, the General's widow and I will have a private talk (when it suits her, as I am never pressed for time) about certain insignificant details of procedure which will give a natural or reasonable aspect to what will always basically be a great act of charity on her part. And now that I have explained, in this long speech, for which I did not come prepared, all aspects and sides of this matter, I shall now take my seat again. Thank you very much.'

The Captain was still whistling the *Himno de Riego*, and very likely the anthems of Bilbao and Maella, with his angry glance fixed on the ceiling of the bedroom so ferociously that it was a wonder it did not burst into flames or collapse on the floor.

When Angustias and her mother saw that their enemy had been defeated, they tried to attract his attention two or three times so as to calm and console him with gentleness and kindness; but he had replied with bitter and sharp gestures, resembling vows of vengeance and had gone back to whistling patriotic airs even more ardently and jocosely.

He looked very like a madman with his keeper, for that was precisely the role that the Marquess was playing in that room.

CHAPTER 14

Indispensable Preamble

At this point Doctor Sánchez retired from the room. As an experienced physiologist and psychologist, he had grasped and described the patient's entire condition, as if he were dealing with an automaton rather than a man. Then the marquess requested the widow once more to give him a few minutes in private with her.

Doña Teresa took him to her sitting-room, at the other end of the main room, and once the two sexagenarians were comfortably installed in an armchair each, the man, accustomed to public life, began by asking if he could have a glass of sugared water, claiming that it had tired him to speak twice successively ever since he had delivered a three-day speech in the Senate against railways and telegraphs. But what he really wanted when he asked for the water was for the lady from Guipúzcoa to have time to explain all about her status as a general's widow and a countess, about none of which the good Marquess knew anything and which were very important matters, since the question of money was about to be raised.

The reader may well imagine the pleasure with which the poor woman expatiated on the subject, as soon as Don Alvaro gave her the slightest opportunity to do so by asking one or two ever so slightly inquisitive questions! She talked about her *case*, from beginning to end, without forgetting the phrase about *virtual*, *retrospective* and *implicit* rights to enjoy an income, in which she was protected by Article 10 of the Convention of Vergara. And when she had nothing more to say and began to fan herself as a signal of truce, the Marquess de Los Tomillares began to speak . . .

(But it would be better for his interesting statement to be written separately. It was a model of analytical exposition and might well appear in the twentieth part of his works, under the title: *My relatives, friends and servants*.)

CHAPTER 15

The Captain's History

'COUNTESS, you have the ill-fortune to harbour under your roof one of the most contrary and difficult men that God ever created on this earth. I shall not say that he seems just like the Devil, but it is certainly true that one needs to be made of the stuff of angels, or love him, as I love him, by natural law and through pity, to put up with his rudeness, bad temper and mad ways. It is sufficient for you to know that the dissipated and not easily shocked people with whom he associates in the casino and the cafés have nicknamed him Captain Poison when they see that he can kill you with a look and is quite prepared to break anyone's head for a bagatelle. Nevertheless, I should be failing in my duty if I did not tell you, for your own peace of mind and the trust of your family, that he is chaste and a man of honour and self-respect, not only incapable of offending the modesty of any lady but even excessively cold and shy towards the fair sex. I can say even more: for all his perpetual bad temper, he has never yet done any real harm to anybody, except to himself and, as for me, you have already seen that he behaves towards me with the respect and affection owed towards a sort of older brother or adoptive father . . . but, apart from this, I repeat that he is an impossible man to live with, as is demonstrated eloquently by the fact that, though he is single and I am a widower, and neither of us has any family dependants or known or possible heirs, he does not reside in my over-large house, as the stupid boy certainly could if he wanted to, for I am by nature most tolerant, long-suffering and easy-going with people who respect my tastes, habits, ideas, hours, places and interests. It is this very softness in my nature which in any case makes our private lives quite incompatible, as various attempts have already clearly shown; for he cannot endure gentle and courteous manners, tender and affectionate scenes and anything that is not rough, harsh, strong and bellicose. The reason is obvious. He grew up without a mother, and almost without a nurse (his mother died in giving birth to him and his father did not want the bother of dealing with wet-nurses so he found him a goat, apparently a wild one, to give him suck).

'As soon as he was weaned they sent him to boarding school, as his father, my poor uncle Rodrigo, committed suicide shortly after his wife died. The down appeared on his chin when he was fighting in America among savage Indians. After that, he came back here to fight in our Seven Years War.* He would have been a general by now if he had not quarrelled with his superiors ever since he put on the cadet's aglets. The few promotions and posts he has obtained up till now have cost him prodigious acts of valour and heaven knows how many wounds, without which he would never have had his name put forward by his superiors for consideration, seeing that they are always against him because he habitually tells them some very unpleasant truths. He has been under arrest sixteen times and in various military prisons four times, all for insubordination! What he has never done is rise against the Government!

'Since the war ended he's been awaiting posting because though I certainly have managed, while I have been in political favour, to place him here and there in military departments or regiments, twenty-four hours later they've sent him back home! He has challenged two ministers of war to duels and the only reason he hasn't been shot by firing squad yet is out of respect for me and the fact of his undeniable courage. In spite of all these disasters, and in view of the fact that he has gambled away his small capital playing cards at the casino and that his reserve pay while without posting was insufficient for him to live on according to the standards of his social class, seven years ago I had the wonderful idea of making him steward of my house and estate, both having been very speedily disentailed by the successive deaths of the last owners (my father and my brothers Alfonso and Enrique) and very tumbledown and ruined because of these changes of owner. Without

* The Carlist War of 1833-9

any doubt Providence itself inspired that most daring idea! From that day on my affairs fell into order and waxed prosperous; ancient or disloyal administrators lost their jobs or mended their ways and the following year my income had doubled and is now almost four times what it was because of the way Jorge has developed the stock-raising. I can say today that I have the best rams in lower Aragon, all at your service, Señora. All that tearaway has needed to do to produce such astonishing results is to ride around the estates (carrying his sabre like a stick) and one hour in the office every day. He earns a salary of thirty thousand *reales* and I don't give him any more because everything that he has left over after what he spends on food and on his clothes, the only things he needs (and he is most moderate and unextravagant in them), he gambles away at bezique on the last day of every month. It would be best not to speak of his half-pay as an officer, because it's always embargoed for the expenses of some court-martial for failure to show the proper respect for authority. In other words, in spite of everything, I love him and pity him like a bad son ... and because I wasn't able to have a good or bad one in my three marriages, and because in due course he will inherit, I intend to leave him all my much-improved fortune. Of course the stupid boy has no idea of this and God grant he never gets to know it because, if he did, he would resign his post as steward or try to ruin me so that I should never think that he had any personal interest in increasing my income. The poor boy probably thinks, if he judges by appearances and takes any notice of scandalous rumours, that I'm thinking of making a will in favour of a certain niece of my last wife. I leave him in ignorance, for the reason I have given. Can you imagine his rage the day he inherits my round nine million? What a performance he'll put on with the money all over the place! I'm positive that in three months he'll either be Prime Minister or Minister of War or shot by General Narváez! I really should have liked to get him married, to see if matrimony calmed him down and tamed him and I owed it to him, reciprocally, to ensure that the title did not die with him. But Jorge is incapable of falling in love and he wouldn't admit it even if he did, and no woman could live with a bear like him.

'This is an impartial description of our Captain Poison, so I beg you to tolerate him for a few weeks in the certainty that I shall be grateful for everything you ladies do for his health and his life, as if you were doing it for myself.'

As he finished this part of his speech, the Marquess took out and unfolded his handkerchief and wiped his forehead, though he was not perspiring. At once he refolded it symmetrically, put it away in the left back pocket of his frock coat, pretended to sip the sugared water and then spoke, with a change of attitude and tone:

CHAPTER 16

The Widow of The Warlord

'I THINK we should have a talk about a few minor matters, of absolutely no concern, of course, to people of our position, but on which we must touch. Countess, fate has brought into this house, and will prevent from leaving it for forty or fifty days, a man unknown to you, a stranger, a certain Don Jorge de Córdoba, of whom you have never heard and who has a relative who is a millionaire . . . you are not rich, as you have just told me . . .'

'I am!,' interrupted the Basque lady courageously.

'No, you are not! And it does you great honour, for your generous-hearted husband ruined himself defending a most noble cause . . . I, madam, am also something of a Carlist.'

'I wouldn't care if you were Don Carlos himself! Please change the subject or let me end this conversation. Really! I must say! Accept money from somebody merely for fulfilling my Christian duty!'

'But, madam, you are neither a doctor nor an apothecary, nor . . .'

'My purse is all those things for your cousin! The many times that my husband fell wounded defending Don Carlos (except the last time when, doubtless punished because he had already made an agreement with the traitor Maroto, he couldn't find anyone to help him and bled to death in the middle of a wood) he was aided by Navarrese and Aragonese peasants, who refused to take any compensation or gift. I shall do likewise with Don Jorge de Córdoba, whether his millionaire family likes it or not!'

'Nevertheless, Countess, I cannot accept,' declared the Marquess, gratified and irritated at the same time.

'What you will never do is deprive me of the great honour which heaven granted me yesterday. My late husband used to tell me that when a merchantman or warship discovers some ship-wrecked sailor in the wastes of the sea and saves him from death, he is received on board with royal honours, though he may be the commonest of sailors. The crew climbs on to the rigging. A rich carpet is unrolled on the starboard ladder, and the band and drums play the Royal March of Spain . . . do you know why? Because in that shipwrecked sailor the crew see a messenger of Divine Providence, and I shall do the same with your cousin! I shall cast at his feet, not a carpet, but all my poverty as I should my millions if I had them!'

'Madam!' exclaimed the Marquess, openly weeping. 'Allow me to kiss your hand!'

'Dear Mama, please let me kiss you also, I'm so proud,' added Angustias, who had heard the entire conversation from the door of the drawing-room.

Seeing herself so complimented and praised, Doña Teresa also burst into tears. And, as the Galician servant, seeing that the others were crying, did not waste her chances of sobbing either (without knowing why), there was such a mixture of trembling lips, sobs and blessings, that it might be better to go on to the next page rather than have my readers crying their eyes out as well, which would leave me without an audience to whom to continue to tell my poor tale.

CHAPTER 17

Angustias's Suitors

'JORGE!' said the Marquess to Captain Poison, as he entered the bedroom to take his leave, 'I'm leaving now. General Barbastro's widow has not permitted us to pay for even the doctor and the apothecary; this house will be like your mother's, if she were still alive. I shan't say anything to you about your obligations to treat these good ladies with friendliness and good manners in accordance with your real feelings of which I have no doubt, and with the example of good manners and courtesy which I have given you. With the permission of my lady the Countess, I shall come back this afternoon and I shall have clean linen, the more important papers to sign, and cigarettes brought to you. Tell me if you want anything else from your house or mine.'

'I say!' replied the Captain. 'Since you offer, bring me a bit of raw cotton and some smoked glasses!'

'What for?'

'I need the cotton to plug my ears and not have to listen to idle chatter, and the glasses so that nobody can guess the awful things I'm thinking from the expression in my eyes!'

'Go to the devil!' answered the Marquess, unable to keep a straight face, any more than Doña Teresa and Angustias could stop themselves laughing.

And, with that, the potentate took his leave, with the most tender and expressive words, as if he had known and frequented the ladies for a long time.

'A fine man,' exclaimed the widow, looking at the Captain out of the corner of her eye.

'A real gentleman,' said the Galician, stowing away a gold coin that the Marquess had given her.

'A busybody!' grunted the invalid, looking straight at Angustias, who said nothing. 'That's how "ladies" would like men to be! Betrayer, creeping Jesus! Smooth talker! Nancy boy! Goes to tea with nuns! I won't die till I pay him out for the dirty tricks he's played on me today, leaving me in the hands of my enemies. As soon as I'm better, I'll leave him and his office and apply for a job as a convict-prison governor and live with people who won't get on my nerves by showing off how honourable and sensitive they are. Listen here, Señorita Angustias, would you mind telling me why you're laughing at me? Have I got straw in my hair or something?'

'Not at all. I'm laughing to think how ugly you'll look with dark glasses.'

'That's excellent, you won't run any risk of falling in love with me, then,' replied the enraged Captain.

Angustias burst out laughing, Doña Teresa turned crimson with rage and the Galician, unable to keep silent, began to talk at nineteen to the dozen:

'My mistress doesn't fall in love with anybody. Since I've been here she's sent several men about their business: an apothecary in the Calle Mayor, who has a carriage, the lawyer looking after the countess's case, and he's a millionaire, though he's a bit older than you, and two or three hangers-on in the Retiro park!'

'Be quiet, Rosa,' said Doña Teresa sadly. 'Don't you know that the gentleman's only trying to be – nice? Luckily his cousin has already explained everything we need to know about the character of our charming guest. So I'm pleased to see he's in such a good mood. I wish I could joke also but I feel so wretched.'

The Captain had become rather chastened and looked as if he were thinking out some excuse to give mother and daughter. But the only thing that occurred to him to say, with the voice and expression of a bad-tempered child listening to reason, was:

'Angustias, when this damned leg of mine hurts me less, we can play long bezique. Do you think that would be a good idea?'

'I should be highly honoured,' answered the young woman as she gave him the medicine he was due to take at that moment. 'But I'll tell you now, Captain Poison, that I'll score my forty points!'

Don Jorge looked at her with cow-like eyes and smiled sweetly for the first time in his life.

CHAPTER 18

Skirmishes

TWENTY or thirty days went by in conversations and squabbles of this sort. The Captain rapidly regained his health. The wound in his forehead was now only a short scar and the bone in the leg was mending.

'The man's built like a horse,' the doctor was wont to say.

'I'm most obliged, you heavy-handed old saw-bones,' the captain would reply with kindly sincerity. 'When I'm up and about again, I'll have to take you to the bullfight and the cockfights. You're my sort of man! You're a top-notcher when it comes to putting broken bodies together!'

In the end, Doña Teresa and her guest had begun to like each other greatly, even though they were always quarrelling. Every day Don Jorge refused to believe that her status as a general's and marquess's widow had been granted, and this drove the good lady into a bad temper. But straightaway he invited her to come and sit with him in the bedroom and told her that he'd never heard of a general or a count, but he'd often heard people in the civil war talking about *Captain* Barbastro as one of the bravest and most distinguished Carlist leaders and also as one who was most humane and gentlemanly . . . But when he saw that she was depressed and taciturn, because of her worries and the upsets in her health, he restrained himself from making jokes about her case and called her Señora General and Countess with all the naturalness in the world; this at once made her feel better and more cheerful. Sometimes, as he was Aragonese by birth and in order to remind the poor widow of her love for the dead Carlist, he would hum the typical *jotas* of Aragón, and in the end she perked up and wept and laughed at the same time.

Captain Poison's kindness and, in particular, his singing of the Aragonese *jota*, was a privilege reserved exclusively for Doña Teresa. As soon as Angustias came near the bedroom, they stopped utterly, and the invalid put on his fierce attitude. It was as if he felt a mortal hatred for the pretty young woman, perhaps just because he never managed to pick a quarrel with her, nor saw her at all put out, nor taking seriously the dreadful things he said. Nor could he shake her out of her slightly ironic seriousness which the poor fellow described as a *constant insult*.

All the same, the fact was that, if any morning Angustias was late in coming to wish him good morning, the terrible Don Jorge asked Doña Teresa over and over again in his fierce way:

'What about *her*? Miss makes-me-sick? Where's that lazy girl? I suppose Her Ladyship isn't up yet. Why has she let you get up so early and not brought me my morning chocolate herself? Now tell me, Señora Doña Teresa, is the young Princess of Santurce ill, by any chance?'

All this was directed to the mother. If it was the Galician servant, he spoke even more roughly:

'Now listen and listen properly, you monster from Mondoñedo. Tell your intolerable mistress that it's eight o'clock and I'm hungry. Tell her there's no need to come with her hair all neatly done and shining as she does! In any case I'll hate her with every fibre in my body! And don't forget to say that if she doesn't come there'll be no bezique!'

The bezique was a comedy and even a daily drama. The captain played a lot better than Angustias, but Angustias was luckier and in the end the cards would be thrown up to the ceiling or into the drawing-room by that forty-year-old baby who couldn't endure the charmingly tranquil manner in which the young woman said:

'There, Captain Poison, can't you see I'm the only person in the world who can beat you by forty points?'

CHAPTER 19

The Question is Raised

THAT was the situation when, on the morning of a marvellous Spring day, there was an argument between Don Jorge and his beautiful enemy over whether or not to open the windows in the bedroom. Harsh words were exchanged:

The Captain: 'You drive me mad, you do. You never contradict me and you never get upset at the things I say! You despise me! If you were a man, I swear we'd end up sticking knives into each other!'

Angustias: 'But if I were a man I'd laugh at your bad temper just as I laugh as a woman. All the same, we'd still be good friends.'

The Captain: 'Friends! You and I! Impossible! You've got the infernal knack of annoying me and exasperating me with your good sense. I'd never be your friend, more likely your slave and just so as not to become your slave I'd suggest we fought to the death. That is . . . if you were a man. Since you're a woman . . .'

Angustias: 'Go on then! Please don't spare the gallantry!'

The Captain: 'Yes, ma'am! I'll be perfectly frank with you. I've always had an instinctive aversion for women, the natural enemies of man's strength and dignity. Eve, Armida,* the other hussy who cut off Samson's hair and lots of others that my cousin can quote. But if there's anything that scares me more than a woman, it's a lady, and more than anything, a young lady, innocent and sensitive, with dove's eyes and rose-pink lips, with a body like the serpent in the Garden of Eden and the voice of a siren, with tiny hands as white as lilies, hiding tiger's claws, and crocodile tears which could deceive and be the perdition of all the saints in heaven. So my rule has always been to run away from you. Because, tell me now, what arms does a man have to deal with a twenty-year-old

* Temptress in Tasso's *Gerusalemme Liberata*.

tyrant like you, whose strength lies simply in her own weakness? Is it decently possible to strike a woman? No, of course not! Well then, what can a man do when he learns that some half-baked kid or other, very pretty and nicely turned-out, can manage him and run his life and take him here and there like a lap-dog?'

Angustias: 'Just what I do when you say those dreadful things to me, thank you for them! And smile! You must have noticed that I'm not given to crying, so in your portrait of the Angustias of the world there was no need to mention crocodile tears . . .'

The Captain: 'There you are! The devil himself wouldn't have thought of that answer. Smile! Laugh at me! That's what you do all the time. All right then! I was saying, when you drove that new knife into the wound, that of all the nice young ladies that I was afraid I might meet in the world, the most terrible, the most odious for a man of my sort – please excuse my being frank – is you! I can't remember ever having been so angry as when you smile at me when I'm in a temper. It's as if you doubt my courage, that I'm serious when I shout, or that I'm sincere.'

Angustias: 'Now listen to me now and believe me. This is in all seriousness. I've met many men. More than one has made advances, but none has attracted me so far . . . but if in time I ever fall in love, it would be with some hothead like you. Your character is made to fit mine!'

The Captain: 'Go to hell! Señora! Countess! Call your daughter and tell her not to excite me! I think we'd better not play bezique today. I know you're too good for me. I've sometimes lain awake all night, thinking about our rows and the hard things you make me say, the irritating witticisms you answer me with and about how you and I could never live in peace together in spite of my gratitude to . . . this house, of course. God! It would have been better if you'd let me die in the street! It's very sad to hate or not be able to behave properly toward the person who saved my life nearly at the cost of her own! Thank heavens, it won't be long before I'll be able to move this wretched leg. I'll go to my little room in the Calle de Tudescos, my self-contented relative's office and my

dear casino and that'll be an end to this torment to which
you've submitted me with your angel's face, body and movements, and your devil's coldness, humour and smiles! We
shan't be seeing each other soon! I'll think of some way of
speaking to your mother alone, either at my cousin's house, or
by letter, or arranging to meet at some church or other . . .
but as far as you are concerned . . . my dear . . . I shan't go
near you again until I hear you're married! In other words . . .
leave me alone! Or put poison in my chocolate tomorrow!'

The day Don Jorge de Córdoba uttered these words,
Angustias did not smile, but grew grave and sad. The Captain
observed this and hastily covered his face with bedclothes,
muttering to himself:

'I've spoilt it for myself by saying I didn't want to play
bezique. But I can't change my mind now. It'd be demeaning
myself. Too bad. Swallow your bile, Señor Captain Poison!
Men must be men!'

Angustias had already left his room and did not notice the re-
pentance and sadness struggling beneath the sheets of that bed.

CHAPTER 20

Convalescence

A FURTHER fortnight passed without anything of particular
note happening. The day arrived when our hero was due to
leave his bed, though he had strict orders not to move from a
chair and to keep his injured leg stretched out on another.

The Marquess de los Tomillares had not failed to visit Don
Jorge one single morning, or perhaps it should be said that he
had visited his charming nurses, with whom the Marquess got
on much better than with his prickly and bad-tempered
cousin. When he heard about Don Jorge's requirements, he
sent him at dawn a magnificent invalid-chair made of oak,
steel and damask, which he had ordered to be constructed
some time before.

That luxurious item of furniture was a work of art, carefully thought-out and supervised by the diligent nobleman. It had large wheels which would make it easier to take the invalid here and there and it was jointed with a large number of springs. This allowed it to adopt the form of a camp bed, or a more or less reclining armchair. In the latter case it had a support for his right leg. It also had a side-table, a lectern, a writing desk, a mirror and many other adjustable pieces, all extremely well fitted.

He sent the ladies some most elegant bunches of flowers, as he did every day, and besides, as this was a special day, he sent a large box of pastries and a dozen bottles of champagne to celebrate the recovery of their guest. He presented a handsome watch to the doctor and twenty-five *duros* to the servant. And so a very happy day was spent in that house, although Doña Teresa's health was getting steadily worse.

CHAPTER 21

A Look Back

THE fact is that ever since the famous argument about the fair sex, the Captain had changed slightly, not in his habits or manners, but at least in his temper . . . and perhaps even in his ideas and feelings. It was evident that ladies caused him less annoyance than previously and everybody noticed how trusting and kind he was to the Señora de Barbastro, a kindness which was showing through in his relationship with Angustias.

Of course he went on saying that she was his mortal enemy and speaking, or rather shouting at her with apparent harshness as if he were ordering soldiers, probably through Aragonese obstinacy more than anything else. But he watched her wherever she went and gazed at her with respect. If by any chance his eyes met those of the fearless and mysterious young woman (who had been growing steadily more serious and sad since that famous day) he seemed to yearn to inquire the reason for her seriousness and sadness.

Angustias, for her part, had ceased to provoke the Captain

and smile at him when she saw he was flying into a rage. She attended him in silence and in silence tolerated his more or less bitter and genuine irritation, until he also grew serious and sad and asked her with something of the frankness of an innocent child,

'What's the matter? Are you angry with me? Are you beginning to have your revenge for the hatred I talked so much about to you?'

'Let's not talk nonsense, Captain,' she replied, 'both of us have already made sufficient fools of ourselves . . . talking about very serious things.'

'So, do you admit that you're beating a retreat?'

'Retreat? From what?'

'Come on . . . you know. Didn't you make out you were brave and a fighter the day you called me a wild Indian?'

'Yes, and I don't regret it, my friend . . . but that's enough nonsense. It's time for you to go to sleep.'

'Are you going? That's not fair! That's running away!' the Captain would say to her craftily.

'If you say so,' Angustias replied, shrugging her shoulders, 'but the fact is I'm going to my room.'

'And what am I going to do here all night! It's only seven, you know!'

'That's of no interest to me. You can say your prayers, or go to sleep or talk to Mama . . . I've got to get on with putting some order into the trunkful of papers which belonged to my late father. Why don't you ask Rosa for a pack of cards and play solitaire?'

'Tell me frankly,' the persistent bachelor asked one day as his greedy eyes devoured the white and dimpled hands of his antagonist. 'Are you still angry with me because we haven't played bezique since that morning?'

'Quite the contrary! I'm very happy we've stopped that nonsense!' answered Angustias, plunging her hands into the pockets of her housecoat.

'Then, for God's sake, what do you want?'

'I don't want anything, Señor Don Jorge.'

'Why don't you call me Señor Captain Poison any more?'

'Because I've realized that you don't deserve that name.'

'Hullo, Hullo, we've got back to fine words and praises. I see. How do you know what I'm really like?'

'What I do know is that you'll never get as far as poisoning anyone.'

'Why? Am I too cowardly?'

'No, sir, because you're a poor man, with a very good heart, which you seem to have tied up with a chain and a bit, maybe through pride or because you're afraid of your own sensitivity . . . if that's not true, ask my mother.'

'Eh, what? Let's leave that. Hide your flattery as you hide your little ivory hands, if you please! The child wants to turn me inside out!'

'It would do you a great deal of good if I had that idea and managed it, because inside-out for you is the right way round! But that's not the question. Your affairs are no concern of mine!'

'God Almighty! Why didn't you tell yourself that on the day you got a bullet through your skirt saving my life?' exclaimed Don Jorge so forcibly that it was as if a bomb rather than gratitude had exploded in his breast.

Angustias looked at him happily and said with noble pride and energy:

'I don't regret what I did, because if I admired you when I saw you fighting on the afternoon of March the twenty-sixth I admired you even more when I heard you singing the Aragonese *jota*, though you were in severe pain, just to calm and please my poor mother.'

'Yes, that's right. Go on, sneer at my bad voice!'

'Lord, what a terrible man! I'm not sneering at you, nor is there anything to sneer at. I have been almost in tears and I have blessed you from afar, every time I heard you singing those verses!'

'Snivelling! It's worse and worse! Señora Doña Angustias, I'll have to be very careful with you! You've taken it into your head to make me say things which are ridiculous and fatuous for a man of character like me, just so as to be able to laugh at me later and say you've won the battle! Fortunately, I'm on my guard and as soon as I see I'm about to fall into the trap, I'll run, with my broken leg and all, and I shan't stop until I get to Peking! You must be what they call a flirt!'

'And you're a wretch!'

'That's how I like it!'

'You're unjust, ill-mannered and stupid!'

'Go on! Go on! That's how I like it! At last we are going to have a fight!'

'You're ungrateful!'

'Oh no, by heck, oh no, I'm not!'

'Very well, then, keep your gratitude. Thank God, I don't need it. But most important, please kindly refrain from drawing me into these conversations again.'

Those were Angustias's words, and she turned her back on him in real anger.

And so darkness and confusion still obscured the most important question which, without knowing it, those two people had been arguing about since they first saw each other . . . and which very soon would become as clear as day.

CHAPTER 22

An Unforeseen Accident

THE famous and joyful day on which Captain Poison was able to get up was to have a rather sad and unfortunate end, as so often happens in this vale of tears, as we wrote philosophically some time before and for quite opposite reasons to the ones in this case.

Night was falling, the doctor and the Marquess had just left and Angustias and Rosa had also gone out, on the advice of Doña Teresa, who was very happy, to say a *Salve* to the Virgin of the Good Tidings, when the Captain, who had been put to bed again, heard the streetbell ring.

He heard Doña Teresa open the peep-hole and ask:

'Who is it?' and then say as she opened the door:

'How on earth could I imagine you would come at this time of day? Come this way.'

Then a man's voice said, fading as he went into the inner room, 'I'm most sorry, Señora . . .'

The rest of the sentence was lost in the distance and there was silence for a few minutes and then steps were heard again and the same man's voice, as if saying good-bye:

'I hope you get better and feel easier in yourself . . .' Doña Teresa replied:

'Please don't worry . . .' after which the door was heard to open and close again and profound silence pervaded the house.

The Captain realized that something unpleasant had happened to the widow and he even expected that she would come in and tell him about it; but when it seemed that this would not happen he deduced that the matter was a domestic secret and he refrained from calling out to her, though he thought he could hear her sighing in the corridor close by.

At that moment there was nother ring at the street door and Doña Teresa opened it at once, which proved she had not moved since her visitor had left. Then he heard Angustias exclaim:

'Why were you waiting for us with your hand on the latch? Mama! What's the matter? Why are you crying? Why don't you answer me? Are you ill? Oh my God! Rosa! Go, run and fetch Doctor Sánchez! My mother's dying! Come here! Wait! Help me to put her on the sofa in the living-room . . . can't you see she can't stand? Oh, Mother darling! What's the matter! Why can't you walk?'

And, in fact, she could not. From his bedroom Don Jorge saw Doña Teresa being almost dragged into the drawing-room hanging on the necks of her daughter and Rosa, and with her head sunk on her breast.

Then Angustias remembered that the Captain was there and uttered a cry of rage. She faced him squarely and said:

'What have you done to my mother?'

'No, no, poor man, he doesn't know anything about it!' the sick woman said hastily in a tender tone. 'I became ill by myself, but I'm beginning to feel better now.'

The Captain was red with indignation and embarrassment:

'Now, you can hear, can't you, Señorita Angustias?' he exclaimed at last in a very bitter and sad voice. 'You've slandered me very cruelly! No, no, I've slandered myself ever since I've been here! I deserve the injustice you do me! Doña Teresa! Take no notice of this ungrateful girl and tell me you're quite all right now or I'll go mad here and now where I'm tied down with pain and crucified by my enemy!'

During all this, the widow had been settled on the sofa and Rosa was crossing the street to fetch Dr Sánchez.

'I'm sorry, Captain,' said Angustias, 'you must realize that she's my mother. Now I found her dying not far away from you, when I left her by your side a quarter of an hour ago . . . did anyone come while I was away?'

The Captain was about to reply that somebody had come when Doña Teresa interrupted him and said hurriedly:

'No, nobody! Isn't that so, Señor Don Jorge? All this is nerves, the vapours, old woman's trouble, that's all. I'm well now, Angustias, dear.'

Don Jorge was sweating with pain.

When the doctor came he took the widow's pulse. He had left her half-an-hour before very happy and almost normal in health. He then said that she should be put to bed at once and stay there for some time until the great nervous commotion she had suffered was dispelled. Then he told Don Jorge and Angustias in confidence that Doña Teresa's illness was in the heart. He had been sure of this since he had taken her pulse for the first time on the afternoon of the twenty-sixth of March. Illnesses of the sort, though not easy to cure completely, could be tolerated for a long time provided the patient rested, was well looked-after, kept moderately happy, was cared for, and lots of other marvels, the main basis of which was money.

'March the twenty-sixth,' muttered the Captain. 'In other words, I'm to blame for everything that's happening.'

'No, the blame is mine!' said Angustias, as if to herself.

'Don't look for the cause of causes!' observed Doctor Sánchez gloomily. 'Before there can be any blame there has to be intention and you're quite incapable of having meant to harm Doña Teresa.'

Freed from blame, the two looked at each other with angelic expressions of surprise on their faces, to see that science was racking its brain to come to such obvious or impious deductions. Then, putting their minds to what really mattered at the moment, they said to each other at the same time,

'We must save her!'

And that was the beginning of an understanding.

CHAPTER 23

Catastrophe

As soon as the doctor left, a long debate took place. They decided to put the widow's bed in the study which, as explained before, led off one end of the drawing-room, exactly opposite the bedroom occupied by Don Jorge.

'Like that,' said Angustias, ever thoughtful, 'you two invalids can see each other and talk, and it will be easier for Rosa and myself to attend to you from the main room on the night each one of us has to stay awake and watch you.'

That night Angustias stayed with them and nothing untoward happened. At dawn Doña Teresa grew very calm and dozed for about an hour. The doctor thought she was much better when he came in the morning. As she was very calm throughout the next day as well, on the second night Angustias went to her own room at about two in the morning, in obedience to the tender supplications of her mother and the imperious commands of Don Jorge. Rosa stayed as night nurse . . . in the same armchair, in the same position and emitting the same snores as on the day that the Captain was wounded.

It must have been about half past three in the morning when our captious hero, unable to sleep, heard Doña Teresa breathing with difficulty and calling him in a lifeless and faltering voice.

'Neighbour, are you calling me?' asked Jorge, hiding his anxiety.

'Yes. Captain,' replied the sick woman, 'wake up Rosa, but carefully, so that my daughter doesn't hear. I can't raise my voice any more . . .'

'But what's the matter? Do you feel ill?'

'Yes, very ill. And I want to speak to you alone before I die . . . tell Rosa to sit you in the wheelchair and bring you here . . . but make sure she doesn't wake up my poor Angustias . . .'

The Captain did exactly what the old lady wanted and very soon he was by her side.

The poor widow had a high fever and was finding difficulty in breathing. On her livid face the indelible sign of death was already evident.

The Captain was afraid for the first time in his life.

'Go away, Rosa . . . but don't wake up Señorita Angustias. (Please God I live till daybreak and then I'll call her for a last farewell.) Listen, Captain, I'm dying!'

'Of course you are not dying, Señora,' replied Don Jorge, clasping the sick woman's burning hand. 'This is just an attack like the one you had yesterday afternoon. In any case, I don't want you to die!'

'I'm dying, Captain, I know I am. It wouldn't be any good calling the doctor. We must fetch the confessor, yes, even if it does frighten my poor child. But that's after you and I have had a talk. That's the most vital thing now; you and I must talk without anybody to hear us.'

'Well, we're talking now,' answered the Captain, brushing up his moustaches, a sure sign that he was afraid. 'You can ask me for the little and bad blood that I brought into this house and the abundant and first-class blood I've made while I've been here and I'll shed it all with pleasure.'

'Yes, I know . . . I know, my dear friend . . . you are very honourable and you love us . . . very well then, my dear Captain, I shall tell you everything . . . yesterday evening my attorney came and explained that the Government had turned down my application for a pension as the widow of a count and a general.'

'The hell they did! And you got upset about that trifle? I'd like a peseta for every application of mine that the Government's turned down!'

'I'm neither a countess nor a general's widow,' she went on. 'You were right when you said I didn't have those titles.'

'Better still! I'm not a general nor a marquess and my grandfather was both! So now we're equal.'

'Yes, but the fact is that I . . . I'm absolutely ruined. My father and my husband spent everything they had defending Don Carlos. Up till now I've lived on what my jewels have fetched and I sold the last one a week ago . . . a lovely pearl necklace. I'm ashamed to mention these things to you!'

'Go on, Senora, go on talking! We've all had bad times. If you knew the spots I've got into because of that damned bezique!'

'But my spot . . . nothing can be done about it. All my money and my daughter's future was based on the expectation of that widow's pension, which in time would have been Angustias's orphan pension. But now . . . the poor child can't . . . because I'll have to tell you, the lawyer who was advising me was deeply hurt because the child scorned his advances and he wants to make our situation worse so as to break her will and force her to marry him, so last night he sent me the bill for his fees and at the same time as I had that piece of news, my attorney brought me his bill and spoke to me in terms so cruel, repeating what the lawyer had said, using words like "distrust", "insolvency", "execution" and lots of others, that my mind went quite blank and I lost control, opened the cash-box and gave him everything he asked me for, I mean, everything I had left, what I'd been given for my pearl necklace, my last money, the last piece of bread. So, since last night, Angustias is just as poor as those wretched women who beg at doors . . . and she doesn't know! She's sleeping quite peacefully now . . . so of course I don't want to go on living. The strange thing is that I didn't die last night!'

'Well you don't die through little things like that!' retorted the captain, who was sweating with fear but nobly trying to be hearty. 'You did very well to tell me about it. I shall sacrifice myself and live here, surrounded by women, like a butler in a convent. It's my fate! When I'm better I shan't go home but I'll bring my clothes, my weapons and my dogs here and we'll all live together until the world ends . . .'

'Together . . .' replied the lady sadly. 'Can't you see that I'm dying? Can't you see? Do you think I should have told you about my financial problems if I weren't sure of being dead within a few hours?'

'Then, Señora, what do you want me to do?' asked Don Jorge de Córdoba, with horror in his voice. 'Because it's obvious that just to do me the honour and give me pleasure by asking me or requesting me to ask my cousin for that dross they call money, you wouldn't be in such a state, since you know how much we think of you and knowing us . . . as I believe you know us . . . you'll never lack for money so long as I live! Therefore, you want something else of me and I beg of you, before you say another word, to think of the gravity of the circumstances and other things which are also important.'

'I don't understand you, nor do I know what I want myself,' replied Doña Teresa, with the sincerity of a saint. 'But put yourself in my place. I am a mother. At the time of my death I can't see at my side nor have I on the face of the earth anybody else to whom I can entrust her except you, who, in spite of everything, show her some regard . . . honestly, I don't know how you could help her exactly. Money alone is very cold, repugnant, horrible! But it's even more horrible to think of my poor Angustias having to earn her living by working, or as a servant, or begging. So I think I'm justified, as I'm dying, in calling you to bid you farewell, and, with my hands clasped and weeping for the last time in my life, in saying to you from the edge of the grave, Captain, be a guardian, be a father, be a brother to my poor orphaned girl! Help her! Succour her! Defend her life and her honour! Don't let her starve or pine to death! Don't let her be alone in the world! Imagine you have a new daughter from today!'

'Thank God!' exclaimed Don Jorge, thumping the arms of his wheel-chair. 'I'll do all that for Angustias and much more. But I've had a few very nasty moments. I thought you were going to ask me to marry the girl!'

'Señor Don Jorge de Córdoba? No mother can ask that! Nor would my Angustias allow me to dispose of her noble and valiant heart!' said Doña Teresa with such dignity that the captain grew stiff with fright.

The poor chap recovered himself quickly and explained with the humility of the most devoted of sons, kissing the dying woman's hands.

'I'm sorry, I'm sorry, Señora. I'm a fool, a monster, an ill-bred man who can't express himself. I had no intention of offending you or Angustias ... what I wanted to tell you honestly is that I'd make her very unhappy. She's a beautiful young woman, the model of virtue, and I'd make her very unhappy if I did marry her. I wasn't born to love and be loved or to live with anybody or have children or to be sweet, gentle and affectionate ... I'm independent, like a savage, like an animal, and the yoke of matrimony would humiliate me, and I'd kick against the traces. In any case, she doesn't love me, and I don't deserve her and we shouldn't be talking about it at all. But, please believe me, by this first tear that I've shed since I became a man and these first kisses of my lips, that everything I can arrange, my care, my vigilance and my blood, will be for Angustias, whom I respect and love and adore, and to whom I owe my life and even perhaps my soul! I swear it by this holy medallion which my mother always wore around her neck. I swear by ... but ... you can't hear me? You don't answer! You're not looking at me! Do you feel worse? Oh my God! I think she's dead! Damn and blast it! And I can't move! Rosa! Rosa! Water! Vinegar! A confessor! A cross and I'll commend her soul as best as I can! But here's my medallion! Holy Virgin! Receive my second mother! Oh God! Poor Angustias, what about me? Look what's happened to me because I went out to hunt revolutionaries!'

All those exclamations were unfortunately very fitting for the occasion. Doña Teresa had died as she felt the kisses and tears of Captain Poison on her hand, a smile of ecstatic contentment still hovered over the half-open lips of her lifeless body.

CHAPTER 24

Miracles of Sorrow

ANGUSTIAS was awakened by the cries of her badly shaken guest followed by the pitiful 'ays' of the maid. She half-dressed, gripped in the chill hand of fear, and ran to her mother's room . . . but she found the door blocked by Don Jorge's wheel-chair on which he was sitting, with his arms outstretched and his eyes almost out of their sockets, blocking her way and saying,

'Don't go in, Angustias! Don't go in or I'll get up, even if I die!'

'My poor Mama! Darling Mama! Let me see my mother!' moaned the unfortunate girl, fighting to enter the room.

'Angustias! For God's sake, don't go in now! We'll all go in together in a moment . . . let her rest a moment, she's suffered so much!'

'My mother's dead!' exclaimed Angustias, falling on her knees by the Captain's wheel-chair.

'Poor child! Cry as much as you like, here next to me!' replied Don Jorge, drawing the poor orphan's head to his heart, and stroking her hair with his other hand. 'Weep with a man who has never wept until today and weeps for you . . . and for her!'

That emotion was so extraordinary and remarkable in a man like Captain Poison that, in the midst of her awful tragedy, Angustias could only show her gratitude and appreciation by laying one hand on his heart.

And so these two people, whom happiness would never have brought together, remained for some moments in close embrace.

CHAPTER 25

How the Captain Came to Talk to Himself

A FORTNIGHT after Doña Teresa Carrillo de Albornoz had been buried, at about eleven o'clock on a splendid morning in the month of flowers, the eve or two days before Saint Isidore's Day, our friend Captain Poison was swiftly walking through the main room of the house of mourning, supported by two handsome and unusual crutches of ebony and silver, a present from the Marquess de los Tomillares. Although the pampered convalescent was alone and there was nobody in the parlour or in the bedroom, he spoke from time to time in a low voice, with his usual fury and asperity:

'Yes! There, then . . . you can see!' he exclaimed at last, stopping in the middle of the room. 'That's all there is to say! I can walk perfectly! I even think I could walk better without these lumps of wood! I mean I can go back to my own place now . . .'

He blew out his cheeks violently, as if this were his way of sighing, and muttered in a different tone of voice,

' "I can", I said "I can" . . . What does that mean, "can"? I used to think a man could do anything he wanted but now I can see that he can't even *want* what suits him . . . Damn women! Wasn't I right to be wary of them all my life? And I knew exactly what would happen when I saw skirts all around me on the night of March the twenty-sixth. Your having me suckled by a goat, father, was a useless precaution! After so many years, I've fallen into the clutches of these fiends in skirts who forced you to kill yourself! Ah, yes, but I'll get away, even though I leave my heart in their claws!'

Then he looked at his watch, sighed again and said very quietly, as if keeping it from himself:

'It's a quarter past eleven. I still haven't seen her, though I've been up since six. What times they were when she used to bring me my chocolate and we played bezique! Whenever I ring now the Galician comes . . . may that "worthy servant" as my fool of a cousin would say, drop dead one day! But then, it'll be twelve o'clock and she'll be there. Like a statue dressed in mourning. She doesn't talk, doesn't laugh, doesn't cry, eat, drink and know anything of what's happened, anything of what her mother told me that night, anything of what will happen if God doesn't step in and help ... she's very proud and she imagines the house is hers and all she cares about is my getting better again and going so that my presence here doesn't make people talk. Poor child! How can I tell her her mistake? How can I tell her that she is living in an illusion, that her mother didn't leave her any money, and that everything that's been spent here in the last fortnight has come out of my own pocket? Oh no! I couldn't tell her! I'd rather die than tell her that! But, what can I do? Sooner or later, I'll have to give her an account of some sort, true or false. I can't go on like this for ever. She would never allow it! She'll ask for accounts when she calculates that we've spent the money she assumes her mother left and then we'll have the most almighty row!'

Don Jorge's thoughts had reached this point when there were a few taps on the main door of the room and he heard Angustias's voice:

'May I come in?'

'Yes, come in, with five thousand cavalry if you like!' shouted the captain, crazy with joy, and ran and opened the door, and, forgetting all his alarm and thoughts:

'It's high time you paid me a visit like you used to do. Look at me here! I'm like a bear in a cage, fed up and looking for someone to fight with! Shall we play a hand of bezique? But, what's the matter? Why are you looking at me like that?'

'Let's sit down and talk, Captain,' said Angustias gravely. Her bewitching face was as pale as wax and expressed deep emotion.

Don Jorge gave a twist to his moustaches, as he always did when a storm was in the offing, and sat on the edge of an armchair, looking left and right as nervously as a condemned criminal in chapel just before execution.

The young woman sat down very near him. She thought for a few moments, or rather gathered her forces for the storm which was about to break and then began to speak in a tone of inexpressible gentleness.

CHAPTER 26

The Battle Rages

'Señor de Córdoba. The day my sainted mother died and when, giving in to your insistence, I went to my room after having wrapped her in her winding-sheet, because you insisted in staying there to watch over her body, with a piety and respect that I shall never forget . . .'

'Come on, Angustias, come on then! Who's afraid? Keep a brave face! You must be strong and get over all that!'

'You know that I've never been afraid . . !' replied the young woman more calmly. 'But I'm not talking about the loss, with which I live and shall always live in holy resignation and which is so sweet that I would not give it up for anything in the world. I'm talking about irritating things of quite another type where, thank heavens, changes can be made and are going to be made completely and at once . . .'

'Please God!' prayed the Captain, seeing the black clouds coming nearer.

'I was saying,' went on Angustias, 'that the morning you spoke to me, using more or less these words, "my child" . . .'

'By George! The things one does say! I called you "my child"?'

'Please let me continue, Don Jorge. "My child" . . . you exclaimed with a voice that touched the depths of my being. "You shouldn't think of anything now except to weep and pray God for your mother's soul . . . you know I stayed with that most holy woman in her last moments. And so I found out about all her circumstances. She handed me the money she possessed so that I should attend to the funeral, the mourning clothes and the rest, as your guardian, which she had appointed me privately so that you should not have any worries in the first few days of your sorrow. When you feel a little easier, we'll settle accounts." '

'So?' interrupted the Captain, frowning violently as if by

assuming a ferocious expression, he were trying to change the nature of things. 'Haven't I fulfilled my obligations properly? Have I done anything stupid? Do you think I frittered away your inheritance? Wasn't I right to have a first-class funeral for the noble lady? Or perhaps some gossip has told you already that I had the words Marchioness and widow of the General engraved on the big tombstone I had put there? Well, the stone was a personal wish of mine and I thought I'd ask you to let me pay for it with my own money! I couldn't resist the temptation to give my noble friend the pleasure and the pride of using among the dead those titles which she was not allowed to have among the living.'

'I didn't know about the tombstone,' said Angustias with adoring gratitude, clasping and squeezing one of Don Jorge's hands, in spite of his efforts to pull it away. 'May God reward you for it! I accept this present, in my mother's name and in my own. But, even so, you did wrong, very wrong, in deceiving me in other matters. If I had realized it before, I should have asked for an explanation!'

'And would you mind telling me, my dear young lady, just in what way I have deceived you?' Don Jorge dared to question her still, not imagining that Angustias knew things that Doña Teresa had told only him, and a few minutes before she died.

'You deceived me on that unhappy morning,' the young woman replied in a severe tone of voice, 'when you told me that my mother handed over some sum or other of money to you . . .'

'And what gives Your Ladyship the right to the insolence to accuse a captain in the Army of lying? I'm an honourable man, and I'm older than you!' shouted the Captain with feigned fury, trying to cheapen the matter and put on a show of quarrelling to conceal the mess he was in.

'My right,' replied Angustias calmly, 'comes from the fact that I found out for certain later that when my mother took to her bed she had no money at all.'

'What do you mean, no money at all? These girls think they know everything! But don't you know that Doña Teresa had just sold a jewel of great value?'

'Yes, yes, I know that, a pearl necklace with a diamond clasp . . . for which she received five hundred *duros* . . .'

'Precisely. A necklace of pearls like nuts and we still have a lot of money to spend from what she obtained for it. Do you want me to hand it over to you here and now? Do you want to take over the running of your estate already? Does my being your guardian suit you so ill?'

'How good you are Captain! But you are also so imprudent at the same time,' countered the young woman. 'Read this letter which I have just received and you'll see where the five hundred *duros* actually were, beginning on the evening my mother collapsed with a death wound in her heart . . .'

The Captain turned redder than a beetroot, but still he made a tremendous effort and exclaimed with feigned rage:

'So you mean to say that I'm lying! So a scrap of paper has more credit than me! So a life of decent behaviour where my word was my bond, is worth nothing!'

'Don Jorge, what it is worth is that I thank you over and over and over again because it was for me and for me alone, that you failed to tell the truth just for once.'

'Let me see what the letter says!' retorted the Captain, to see if he could find in it some way of righting the situation. 'It's probably some rubbish or other.'

The letter was from the lawyer or adviser of the late General's widow and read as follows:

Señorita Doña Angustias Barbastro,

Dear Madam and my dear friend,

I have just unofficially received the sad news of the passing away of your lady mother (may she rest in peace) and I offer my sympathy in your distress, wishing you the moral and physical strength to endure such a final and cruel blow from the power which regulates human destinies. Having said this, which is not a formula, or mere expression of courtesy, but the expression of the long and close affection which I have for you, I must fulfil another sacred duty, that is the following.

The broker or business agent of your mother told me the sad news today and at the same time said that, when two weeks ago he informed her of the adverse decision on her application for her widow's pension and when he presented several bills for our honoraria, he was in a position to note that the lady possessed hardly enough money to satisfy them, though she paid them on the spot, with a haste in which I thought I could see fresh indications of the imbalance which you had spoken to me about on previous occasions. With this in mind, my dear Angustias, I am tormented by the thought that you might be having difficulties and facing problems in such aggravating circumstances because of the unnecessary haste with which your mother paid that sum (a low price for the six applications, the drafts of which I wrote for her and even made fair copies of) and I beg you to allow me to return the money and also to add whatever else you need and I possess.

It is no fault of mine if I do not possess sufficient name or any other titles than a love which is as great as it is unrequited, when I make you this offer that I beg you to accept in due form from your devoted and faithful friend, your attentive and sure servant who kisses your feet,

Tadeo Jacinto de Pajares

'There's a lawyer whose throat I'm going to cut!' exclaimed Don Jorge waving the letter above his head. 'What a wretch! What a pig! What a dog! He kills the old lady by talking about *insolvency* and *execution* when he asks for his honoraria, to see if he can force her to make you marry him, and now he wants to buy your hand with the money he got out of her for losing the case about her widow's pension. No, No! I'm off after him! Here! Hand me those crutches! Rosa! My hat! I mean, go to my house and tell them to give it to you. Or if not, bring me (there it is in the bedroom) my officers' cap . . . and my sabre. My crutches are more than enough to break his head with!'

'Go away, Rosa, and don't take any notice. This is just Don Jorge's sense of humour,' explained Angustias as she tore the letter to pieces. 'Now, Captain, sit down and listen to me, please. I despise the lawyer with all his illgotten millions. I haven't answered him and I shall not. He's a coward and a miser and of course he thought he could make a woman like me his merely by defending our bad cause in Government offices. Let's not say anything more, now or later, about that unpleasant old man.'

'Well, I don't want to talk about anything else!' added the

Captain craftily, managing to reach his crutches and beginning to walk fast as if trying to get away from the interrupted argument.

'But, my dear friend,' said the young lady with a voice full of feeling. 'Things can't be left there.'

'Yes, yes, we'll talk about that later! The important thing now is lunch because I'm very hungry indeed. And that clever old fox of a doctor has given me such a strong leg. I can walk like a deer! Tell me, sunshine, what's the date today?'

'Captain!' exclaimed Angustias in an angry tone, 'I shall not move from this chair until you hear me out and we settle the matter which brought me here!'

'What matter? Oh, come now . . . stop harping on that old tune! And talking of tunes, I'll swear I'll never sing the Aragonese *jota* again in my life! Poor Doña Teresa. How she loved to hear me!'

'Señor de Córdoba,' Angustias began again, more cuttingly, 'Again I beg of you to attend to what I am saying because my honour and my dignity are compromised here.'

'Nothing is compromised as far as I am concerned!' replied Don Jorge, flourishing the shorter of his crutches. 'For me you are the most honourable and worthy woman on God's earth!'

'It isn't enough for me to be so for you! Everybody must have the same opinion! So sit down and listen to me, or I'll send for your cousin. He's a man of conscience and he'll put an end to the shameful situation in which I find myself.'

'I shan't sit down, I tell you! I'm fed up with beds, armchairs and chairs. Still, you can speak as much as you want . . .' retorted Don Jorge, stopping his flourishes with his crutch but standing in the position of 'on guard'.

'I shan't say very much,' said Angustias, using her serious voice again, 'and the little I have to say, you've known what it was from the first moment. Señor Captain, you've been maintaining this house for the last fortnight. You paid for my mother's funeral, you paid for the mourning clothes, you gave me the bread I have eaten. At the moment I can't pay you what you have spent, but I shall do so in time, but I'm telling you that from now on . . .'

'Damn and blast! Pay me! She wants to pay me!' shouted the Captain with as much pain in his voice as rage, lifting his crutches high in the air so that the longer one reached the ceiling of the room. 'This woman intends to kill me! And that's why she wants me to listen to her. Well, I shan't listen! The conversation is over! Rosa! Lunch! Señorita, I'll see you in the dining-room. Have the kindness not to make me wait too long.'

'You have a fine way of respecting my mother's memory! You certainly fulfil the obligations she asked of you for her poor orphaned daughter! What great interest you take in my honour and my peace of mind!' exclaimed Angustias with such nobility that Don Jorge was brought up sharp like a reined-in horse. He looked at the young woman for a moment, hurled the crutches away, sat down in the armchair again and said, as he folded his arms:

'Go on, talk until kingdom come.'

'I was saying,' continued Angustias as soon as she had calmed down, 'that this absurd situation which you have created by your imprudent generosity, will stop from today onwards. You are well now and can go back home.'

'A neat solution,' interrupted Don Jorge, placing his hand over his mouth at once as if sorry for the interruption.

'The only one possible,' countered Angustias.

'And what'll you do then, for God's sake?' shouted the Captain. 'Live off air, like a chameleon?'

'Me? I'll be all right. I shall sell the furniture and the linen . . .'

'Which is worth twopence-halfpenny!' the Captain again interrupted, glancing with scorn around the four walls of the room, not in a particularly ruinous state, it must be said.

'Whatever they're worth!' resumed the orphan mildly. 'The point is that I shall stop living at your expense or on the charity of your cousin.'

'Oh no, damn me, oh no! My cousin hasn't paid for any-thing!' roared the Captain nobly. 'That would have been the limit while I was still on this earth. Certainly, poor Alvaro . . . I shouldn't like to deprive him of the credit . . . offered to do anything necessary when he heard the sad news . . . he offered to do much more than you could imagine. But I told him that the daughter of the Countess of Santurce could only accept favours (that is do favours by the mere act of accepting them) from her guardian, Don Jorge de Córdoba, to whose care the dead lady commended her. The man saw reason, and then I lowered myself to ask him to lend me, only lend me, a few coppers on account of the salary I earn in his counting-house. Therefore, Señorita Angustias, you may rest easy on that matter, even though you're prouder than the Empress of of China.'

'It makes no difference,' stammered the girl, 'since I shall have to pay one or the other of you when . . .'

'When what? That's the whole point. Tell me when!'

'I mean . . . when, after working and with the help of All-Merciful God, I can make a way for myself in life.'

'Ways, canals and harbours!' vociferated the Captain. 'Madam, now come on then! Stop talking nonsense! You, work? Work with those pretty little hands that I didn't stop looking at when we used to play bezique! Now what am I in the world for if the daughter of Doña Teresa Carrillo, of my only friend, has to take a needle, or an iron, or a devil, to earn herself a crust of bread?'

'Very well. Let us leave all that to time and for me to think about,' replied Angustias, lowering her eyes. 'But meanwhile we must agree that you should, for my sake, go away today . . . you will go away, won't you?'

'You keep on and on! And why should I! Why should I go away if I like it here?'

'Because you've recovered your health. You can walk along the street just as you can walk around the house. And I don't think it's a good thing that we should go on living together.'

'Well, you'd better imagine that this is a boarding-house then. See, everything's arranged! I'll pay you for my board; you and the maid can look after me, and everybody will be happy! With my two salaries, there's more than enough for all of us to live very well, since I shan't be courtmartialled in the future for disrespect and I shan't lose anything playing bezique, unless it's my temper, when you win one game after the other against me. So we're agreed then, are we?'

'Try to control yourself, Captain,' said Angustias with melancholy in her voice, 'you didn't come into this house as a lodger and nobody would believe you were here as such, nor do I want you to be here. I'm not of an age or nature to be a boarding-house keeper. I prefer to earn a daily wage by sewing or embroidery.'

'And I'd rather be hanged!' shouted the Captain.

'You're very compassionate,' the orphan went on, 'and I thank you from the bottom of my heart that you're suffering to see that you can't help me in any way. But that's life, that's how the world is, that is society's law.'

'What does society matter to me?'

'It matters to me a great deal! Among other reasons because its laws are a reflection of God's laws.'

'So, it's God's law that I can't support whoever I like?'

'It is, Señor Captain, simply because society is divided into families . . .'

'I haven't got a family and so I can do what I like with my money!'

'But I can't accept it. The daughter of a respectable man bearing the name of Barbastro and of a worthy woman who was called Carrillo, cannot live at the expense of just anybody.'

'So, I'm just anybody to you?'

'And the worst sort of anybody . . . for this purpose, since you are a bachelor, still young and not at all of good . . . reputation.'

'Look here, señorita!' exclaimed the Captain, with resolution in his voice, after a brief pause as if he were going to terminate and sum up an intricate argument. 'The night I helped your mother to die in a Christian-like way, I told her openly, and with my usual frankness (so that the good lady should not die under a misunderstanding, but knowing everything that was happening) that I, Captain Poison, would undergo everything in the world except have wife and children. Shall I put it more clearly?'

'What are you telling me for?' replied Angustias with dignity and charm. 'Do you imagine, by any chance, that I'm asking indirectly for your fair hand?'

'No, madam!' Don Jorge hastened to answer, blushing to

the roots of his hair. 'I know you too well to suppose any such idiocy! In any case, we've already seen how you despise millionaire suitors, like the lawyer who wrote the famous letter . . . what am I saying? Doña Teresa gave me the same answer as you when I told her my unbreakable resolve never to marry. But I say this to you, so that you shouldn't think it strange or be offended because, thinking so highly of you as I do (because I love you much more than you imagine) I don't go straight to the point and say "That's enough messing around, darling! Let's get married and live happily ever after!"'

'But it wouldn't be enough for you to say it,' answered the young woman with heroic coolness. 'I should have to like you.'

'Ah, we've got here now, have we?' bellowed the Captain, starting back. 'Perhaps you don't like me?'

'Where on earth did you divine that probability, Don Jorge, sir?' replied Angustias implacably.

'I don't want any of your probabilities or fancy words,' bellowed the poor disciple of Mars. 'I know what I mean! I'll say it quickly and badly. I can't marry you, nor live in your company any other way, nor abandon you to your fate. But believe me, Angustias, you're not a stranger for me, and I'm not one for you . . . and the day I ever learnt that you were working for a wage which meant that you were a servant in somebody else's house, that you were working with your little mother-of-pearl hands . . . that you were hungry or cold or . . . (God, I don't want to even think about it!) I should set fire to Madrid or blow my brains out. So, make a compromise. Since you won't agree to our living together like brother and sister (because people spoil everything with their dirty minds) please let me make you an annual allowance, as kings used to do to people worthy of their protection and aid.'

'But, Don Jorge, the fact is that you are neither a rich man nor a king nor anything like it.'

'No! But for me you are a queen and I must and I want to pay you the voluntary tribute that good subjects used to pay to maintain their banished kings . . .'

'That's enough of kings and queens, Captain.' said Angustias, with quiet resigned despair in her voice. 'You are not nor can ever be for me anything more than an excellent friend from the good old times, whom I shall always remember with pleasure. Let us say good-bye to each other now and please leave me my dignity in my misfortune.'

'Yes, that's right! And I suppose in the meantime I'll bathe in rosewater, knowing that the woman who saved my life by risking her own is having a dreadful time! I shall have the satisfaction of knowing that the only daughter of Eve whom I liked, whom I loved, whom I adore with all my being, lacks the basic necessities, has to work for a poor crust, lives in an attic and receives no aid and no sustenance from me!'

'Señor Captain,' interrupted Angustias solemnly, 'men who cannot marry and have the decency to admit it and proclaim it should not speak to honorable young ladies about adoration. So that's that. Send for a carriage, let's say good-bye like decent people, and you'll have news of me when my fortune changes.'

'Oh my God! What a woman!' exclaimed the Captain, burying his face in his hands. 'I was right to fear it from the moment I laid eyes on her! I must have stopped playing bezique with her for a good reason! There was a reason for lying awake so many nights! Has there ever been a situation so hard as mine now? How can I leave her helpless and alone when I love her more than my own life? But how can I marry her seeing that I have spoken out so often against marriage? What will they say about me in the casino? What will people say when they see me in the street with a woman on my arm, or at home, giving a child his feed? Kids . . . me? Fear every minute that they're ill, that they're dying, that the wind's blowing them away? Angustias, believe me, as Christ is my witness, I'm not cut out for that sort of thing. I would be so unhappy that, so as not to have to listen to me and see me, you'd yell for a divorce or to be left a widow! Take my advice, don't marry me, even though I want you to!'

'But, my dear man,' answered the girl, leaning back in her armchair with admirable serenity. 'You're saying it all yourself. Where do you get the idea that I want us to get married, that I'd accept you if you asked, that I don't prefer living alone, although to do so I should have to work night and day as other orphans work?'

'Where do I get it from?' replied the Captain with the height of ingenuousness, 'from the nature of things! From the fact that we love each other, that we need each other, that there's no other way for a man like me and a woman like you to live together! Do you think I don't know, that I hadn't already thought about it, do you think that your honour and and good name are of no concern to me? But I talked for the sake of talking to escape what I knew, to see if I could get out of the terrible dilemma that is robbing me of sleep, and I found a way of not marrying you, as in the end I shall have to marry you if you insist on staying alone.'

'Alone! Alone!' repeated Angustias pertly. 'And why not better with somebody? What makes you think I shan't find a man whom I like, who does not have a horror of marriage?'

'Angustias, please stop!' shouted the Captain, his face turning the colour of sulphur.

'Stop? Why stop?'

'Stop! I say. And you'd better know now that I'll break the neck of anybody who has the gall to court you ... but it's silly of me to get all worked up for nothing. I'm not so stupid that I don't know what's happening to us. Shall I tell you? Well, it's very simple. We love each other! And don't tell me that I'm mistaken, because that would be untrue. And there's the proof. If you did not love me, I shouldn't love you. What I'm doing is paying back! And I owe you so much! You saved my life and then nursed me like a Sister of Charity. You patiently endured all the dreadful things I said to you for fifty days to free myself from your attraction. You wept in my arms when your mother died and you've been putting up with me for the last hour. So, Angustias, let us compromise! Let's split the difference. I ask you for ten year's grace. When I reach half a century and I'm another man, ill, old and used to the idea of slavery, we'll marry without anyone knowing and we'll go away from Madrid, to the country, where there aren't any people, where nobody can mock the one-time Captain Poison. But, in the meantime, please accept, with the greatest discretion, without a living soul getting to know, half of my resources. You will live here, and I shall live in my home. We'll see each other, but always with somebody there, for example at some proper sort of reception. We'll write to each other every day. I'll never come down this street so that evil tongues won't be able to wag. Only on All Souls' Day we'll go to the cemetery together with Rosa to visit Doña Teresa.'

When Angustias heard the good captain's magnificent speech, she could not help smiling. And it wasn't a mocking smile either. It was joyful, like a longed-for dawn of hope, like the first glint of the long-delayed star of happiness, which was now swimming into her ken . . . but, a woman to the end, though self-respecting and sincere, she said with simulated trust and with the self-confidence natural to a person of modest reserve:

'You really do make the most extraordinary conditions for your unasked-for wedding ring! You're very cruel not to give the needy the alms which they have the pride not to beg for and would not accept for anything on earth! Now it's a young woman you're dealing with on this occasion; she's not ugly or immodest, and you've been pushing her away for the last hour, as if she has been courting you. So, let's put an end to this unpleasant conversation, not without my excusing you first and even thanking you for your kind thought, though it was very badly expressed. Shall I call Rosa and tell her to go and fetch a carriage?'

'Not yet, you obstinate girl! Not yet!' replied the Captain, standing up with a very serious expression on his face, as if he were putting together an abstruse and delicate thought. 'I've just thought of another way of reaching agreement: it'll be the last one, d'you understand? You're obstinate, like all Aragonese. It's the last one that this other Aragonese will be willing to suggest. But before I do so you must give me an honest answer to a question, after passing me my crutches so that I can walk out without another word if you refuse what I'm thinking of proposing to you.'

'Ask your question and make your proposal,' said Angustias, handing him his crutches with a charm and grace impossible to describe.

Don Jorge rested, or rather raised himself on them and, fixing the young woman with a piercing, unwavering and daunting stare, interrogated her like a magistrate:

'Do you like me? Am I acceptable, ignoring these sticks which I'll get rid of very soon? Have we any basis on which to deal? Would you marry me immediately, if I made up my mind to ask for your hand, under the condition which I'll tell you in a minute?'

Angustias knew then that she was playing her last card . . . but even so, she stood up as well and said with unfailing courage:

'Señor Don Jorge. That question is shameful, and no gentleman asks it of any woman he considers to be a lady. I've had enough of this nonsense. Rosa! Señor de Córdoba is calling you!'

And then the generous young girl walked towards the door of the room, after curtseying coldly to the infuriated Captain.

He stopped her half-way, thanks to the longer of the two crutches, which he stretched horizontally as far as the wall, like a gladiator making a thrust, and then exclaimed with unusual humility:

'Please don't go, for the sake of her who is watching us from heaven! I accept that you won't answer my question and I'll now tell you my proposal. It seems to be a law of heaven that you always get your own way! But you, Rosa, clear off and go to the devil, we don't need you here!'

Angustias, fighting to push away the barrier that the Captain had placed between her and the door, stopped when she heard the sincere words he spoke, and looked deeply into his eyes, only turning her head towards him with that indefinable air of superiority, attraction and impassiveness. Don Jorge had never seen her so beautiful and moving. What a queen she looked!

'Angustias,' he went on, or rather stammered on, that hero of a hundred battles, whom the young woman had found so attractive as she saw him struggle like a lion that day among hundreds of bullets, 'on one precise, unchangeable and cardinal condition, I have the honour of requesting your hand in marriage, the date to be chosen by you, tomorrow, today, as soon as we arrange the papers ... as soon as possible. I can't live without you!'

Angustias softened her stare and began to repay Don Jorge for his real heroism with a tender and delightful smile.

'But I repeat that it's under one condition,' the poor man hastened to add, seeing that Angustias's smile and gaze were beginning to disturb and melt him.

'Under what condition?' asked the young woman with bewitching charm, turning round to face him and fascinating him with the torrents of light from her black eyes.

'Under the condition,' stammered the novice, 'that if we have children ... we'll put them into the Foundlings' Home. Now here I'll never give in! Do you accept? For God's sake say yes!'

'But of course I accept, Señor Captain Poison,' replied Angustias, bursting out laughing. 'You can go and put them there yourself! What am I saying? We'll go together! And we'll abandon them without even giving them a kiss! Jorge! Do you think we'll abandon them?'

Those were Angustias's words, as she looked at Don Jorge de Córdoba with an expression of angelic bliss on her face.

The poor Captain thought he'd die of happiness. A river of tears sprang from his eyes and, clasping the gallant orphan in his arms, he exclaimed:

'So I'm lost!'

'Absolutely and thoroughly lost, Señor Captain Poison!' replied Angustias. 'So, let's have lunch, then we'll play bezique, and, in the evening, when the Marquess comes, we'll ask him if he would like to be best man at the wedding, which I'm sure the good gentleman has been wanting ever since the first time he saw us together.'

CHAPTER 27

'Though All Deny Thee . . .'

ONE morning in the month of May, 1852, four years after the scene we have just described, a certain friend of ours (the same who recounted this story to us), stopped his horse at the door of an old palace-like house, situated in the Carrera de San Francisco in our capital city. He handed the reins to a lackey who accompanied him and asked the animated frock coat who came out to the porch to meet him:

'Is Don Jorge de Córdoba in his office?'

'Sir,' answered the above-mentioned piece of cloth in Asturian, 'is asking, I imagine, for the Excelentísimo Señor the Marquess de los Tomillares.'

'What's that? My dear Jorge is a Marquess already?' replied the dismounted rider. 'So good old Alvaro died at last. Don't be surprised that I didn't know because I only arrived in Madrid last night after being away for a year and a half.'

'The Señor Marquess Don Alvaro,' said the servant solemnly, removing the heavily decorated baking-dish which he wore in place of a cap, 'died eight months ago, leaving as his sole and universal heir Don Jorge de Córdoba, the present Marquess de los Tomillares . . .'

'All right. Kindly inform him that his friend T—is here.'

'Please go up. You'll find him in the library. His Excellency does not like visitors to be announced. He likes everybody to walk in and out as if they owned the place.'

'Fortunately,' said the visitor to himself as he climbed the stairs, 'I know the house perfectly, even though I don't own the place. So he's in the library, is he? I never thought Captain Poison would become a scholar!'

When he had walked through several rooms, meeting several servants on his way who said nothing but 'the Señor is in the library', he at last reached the heavily adorned door of the said room, opened it suddenly and stood there stupefied to see the group which appeared in front of his eyes.

In the middle of the room was a man on all fours on the carpet. On top of him was a child about three years old, spurring him on with his heels, and another child about eighteen months old, standing in front of his ruffled head, pulling him by the tie as if it were a halter, and saying rather indistinctly:

'Giddy' up, mule!'

THE RECEIPT BOOK

A country tale

I

THIS story begins in Rota, the smallest of that enchanting group of little townships dotted around the wide arc of the Bay of Cádiz. Yet, even though it is the smallest, someone in the past laid covetous eyes on it. For many years the Duke of Osuna has given it pride of place among the possessions he holds as Duke of Arcos, and there he maintains his palace, which I could describe stone by stone.

But neither palaces nor dukes are to the point here. My subject is the famous country which surrounds Rota, and a very modest market-gardener, whom we shall call old 'Buscabeatas'* though this was not his real name.

The land around Rota, particularly the market-gardens, is so fruitful that not only does it bring the Duke of Osuna many thousands of bushels of grain and supply wine to all the local inhabitants (who are not overfond of drinking-water and very poorly provided with it in any case), but also supplies fruit and vegetables to Cádiz, often to Huelva and even sometimes as far as Seville itself. The region is renowned for its tomatoes and pumpkins whose excellent quality, extreme abundance and consequent cheapness cannot be overstated. That is why, in Lower Andalusia, the people of Rota are nicknamed 'Pumpkineers' or 'Tomato-boys', titles in which they take great pride.

And indeed they have good reason to be proud of these nicknames, for it is true to say that the soil of Rota, so productive (in its market-gardens), yielding sufficient for its own needs as well as for export, giving three or four crops a year, is not soil at all, or anything like it, but pure, clean sand,

* One who looks 'for pious women or nuns'.

ceaselessly thrown up by the turbulent Atlantic Ocean, whirled away by the wild west winds and scattered all over the district, just like the rain of ashes which falls on the villages around Vesuvius.

But Nature's harshness is more than compensated for by Man's constant effort. I know of no farmer, and I doubt if there is any in the world, who works as hard as those of Rota. Not a tiny trickle of fresh water flows through that parched and depressing land . . . what does it matter? The Pumpkineer has literally peppered it with wells, from which, sometimes by manual labour and sometimes by the water-wheel, he extracts the precious substance which is the life blood of vegetables. The sand lacks fertile elements, absorbable humus . . . so what? The Tomato-boy spends half his life seeking and gathering matter which can be used as fertilizer and changing even seaweed into dung! Once he possesses both precious elements, the son of Rota patiently manures, not his entire plot, for he would not have enough fertilizer to do so, but little circles of ground about the size of a small plate, and in each of these manured circles he sows a tomato seed or a pumpkin pip, which he then waters by hand from a diminutive can, like someone giving a drink to a child.

From then until the harvest, every day and one by one, he attends to the plants which are born in those circles, treating them with a tenderness and attention comparable only with the care with which old maids look after their window-boxes. One day he adds a tiny handful of dung to one plant, another gets a little jet of water. Sometimes he removes the snails and other harmful insects from all of them. At other times he looks after sick plants, splinting fractures and putting parapets of reeds and dry leaves around those which cannot endure the rays of the sun or are too exposed to the seawinds, and sometimes, finally, he counts the stalks, the leaves, the flowers or the fruit of the most advanced and forward plants. He speaks to them, caresses, kisses, blesses and even gives them expressive names to distinguish them and give them their own personalities in his mind. This is no exaggeration. There is a proverb, which I have often heard repeated in Rota, which says that the local market-gardener touches each tomato plant at least twenty times with his own hand. And this explains why the old market-gardeners of those parts become so bent that their chins touch their knees!

They have spent all their noble and deserving lives in this posture!

2

Now old Buscabeatas belonged to that group of market-gardeners. He was already beginning to grow bent at the time of the event which I am going to relate. The fact is that he was already sixty years old and had spent forty years working a plot which bordered on the beach of La Costilla.

That year he had grown some marvellous pumpkins, the size of the stone balls on the balustrade of a monumental bridge. They were beginning to turn orange inside and out which meant that the month of June was half-over. Old Buscabeatas knew them perfectly by their shape, their stage of ripeness and even by name, particularly the forty most plump and shiny ones, which were already saying 'cook me'. He spent his days gazing at them tenderly and exclaiming with a melancholy voice:

'Soon we'll have to part!'

Finally, one evening he decided he would make the sacrifice. Selecting the best plants of those beloved *cucurbitae* which had cost him so much effort, he pronounced the dreaded sentence:

'Tomorrow,' he said, 'I shall cut these forty and take them to the market in Cádiz. The people who eat them may consider themselves fortunate!'

And he walked home slowly and spent the night worrying like a father who is going to marry off a daughter the next day.

'What a pity about my pumpkins,' he sighed now and then, unable to fall asleep. But then he reflected and finished by saying:

'And what am I to do except get rid of them? That's what I grew them for! They'll bring me at least fifteen *duros*.'

Imagine, then, his surprise, rage and despair when, the next morning, he went to his plot and found that, during the night, his forty pumpkins had been stolen! To save myself a long description I shall say that, like Shakespeare's Jew, he reached the most sublime height of tragedy, frenziedly repeating those terrible words of Shylock, in which they say the actor Kemble was so magnificent: 'If I can catch him once upon the hip.'

Then old Buscabeatas began to think coolly and realized that his dear darlings could not be in Rota, where it would be impossible to put them on sale without the risk of his recognizing them and where, besides, pumpkins fetch very low prices.

'Yes, I can see it now, they're in Cádiz!' was the result of his meditation. 'The wretch, villain, thief must have stolen them from me at about nine or ten o'clock last night and escaped with them at twelve o'clock in the cargo boat. I'll go off to Cádiz this morning in the hourly boat. I'll be very surprised if I don't catch the thief and recover my babies that I worked so hard to bring up.'

Having pronounced these words, he remained at the scene of the catastrophe for about twenty minutes, as if caressing the mutilated stumps of the pumpkins, or counting the missing ones or preparing a kind of statement of the offence for any case which he thought he might bring. Finally he left for the wharf at about eight.

The hourly boat was already about to sail. This is a humble sailing-boat which leaves every morning for Cádiz promptly at nine, carrying passengers, just as the cargo-boat leaves every night at twelve with fruit and vegetables.

The former is called the hour boat because in an hour, and sometimes in forty minutes, if the wind is from behind, it crosses the three leagues which separate the ancient town of the Duke of Arcos from the ancient city of Hercules.

So it was about half past ten on the morning of that day that old Buscabeatas stopped in front of a vegetable stall in Cádiz market and said to a bored policeman who was walking around with him:

'These are my pumpkins! Arrest that man!'

And he pointed to the stall-keeper.

'Arrest me?' answered the stall-keeper, overcome with astonishment and anger, 'these pumpkins are mine. I bought them.'

'You can tell that to the Mayor,' answered old Buscabeatas.

'No!'

'Yes!'

'You old thief!'

'You villain!'

'Watch your language, you good-for-nothings! Men should not behave like that,' said the policeman very calmly, punching each speaker in the chest.

By this time some people had come up, and before long the alderman in charge of policing public markets, that is to say, the Market Inspector, also made his appearance.

The policeman handed over control to His Honour, and, when this worthy had discovered what was happening, he asked the stall-keeper in a very dignified tone of voice:

'From whom did you buy those pumpkins?'

'Old so-and-so, from Rota,' answered the man.

'It would be him!' shouted old Buscabeatas. 'He's just the sort to do that kind of thing. His land is no good, so, when he can't grow anything, he starts stealing from his neighbour!'

'But, even admitting the hypothesis that you were robbed of forty pumpkins last night,' the alderman went on with his questions, turning to the old market-gardener, 'how can you be sure that these, and none of the others here, are your pumpkins?'

'Oh, now look!' retorted Buscabeatas, 'because I know them as well as you must know your daughters, if you have any. Can't you understand? I raised them. Look. This one is called 'Bouncy', this one 'Chubby', this one 'Tubby', that one 'Rosy-Cheeks' and that one 'Manuela', because it was very like my youngest daughter . . .' And the poor old man began to weep most bitterly.

'Yes, yes, that's all very well,' answered the Market Inspector, 'but the law won't be satisfied just because you can recognize your pumpkins. The authorities must also be convinced of the previous existence of the item in the accusation and it requires you to identify it with satisfactory proofs . . . there's no need to smile, gentlemen, I'm a lawyer!'

'Well, I'll show you and everyone else here and now, without leaving this spot, that those pumpkins were grown in my plot,' said old Buscabeatas, not without great surprise on the part of his audience.

And he put down a bundle which he was holding, stooped and knelt until he was sitting on his feet and calmly began to untie the knotted corner of the handkerchief with which it was wrapped.

The astonishment of councillor, stall-keeper and the circle of idlers reached its apogee.

'What's he going to take out of there?' they all wondered.

At that moment another inquisitive person came up to see what was going on. When the stall-keeper saw him, he exclaimed:

'I'm very happy you've arrived, so-and-so! This man says that the pumpkins you sold me last night and which are here listening to our conversation, are stolen . . . Answer him.'

The newcomer turned whiter than a sheet of paper and tried to make off, but the bystanders prevented him and the alderman himself ordered him to stay.

As for old Buscabeatas, he had faced the presumed thief and said to him:

'Now you'll see something!'

So-and-so recovered his calm and spoke:

'You're the one who should be careful what he says, because if you don't prove, and you can't prove your accusation, you'll be taken to prison as a slanderer. These pumpkins were mine,

I bred them, like all the ones I've brought to Cádiz this year, on my plot on the common, and nobody can prove the contrary.'

'Now you'll see!' repeated old Buscabeatas as he finished untying his bundle and pulled at it.

And then a load of pieces of pumpkin stumps, still green and dripping with juice, tumbled all over the ground, while the old market-gardener, sitting back on his legs and nearly choking with laughter, addressed the following discourse to the councillor and bystanders:

'Gentlemen, have you never paid taxes? And have you never seen that big green book of the collector's, from which he goes around tearing out receipts, leaving a stump or counterfoil so that later it can be proved whether a receipt is false or not?'

'What you are describing is called a receipt book,' observed the alderman gravely.

'Well, that's what I have here: the receipt book of my land, that is the stumps to which these pumpkins were attached before they were stolen from me. If you don't believe me, just look. This stump belonged to this pumpkin . . . nobody can doubt it . . . this one . . . you can see . . . belonged here . . . this wider one . . . must belong to that one . . . exactly! And this one belongs to this one . . . that one to that one. That one to that one over there . . .'

And as he spoke, he fitted a stump or head to the hole which had been left in each pumpkin when it had been pulled out and the astonished spectators saw that, in fact, the bumpy and irregular tops of the stems exactly fitted the white spot and slight hollow presented by what might be called the scars of the pumpkins.

So all the bystanders squatted down, including the policemen and the alderman himself, and began to help old Buscabeatas in his peculiar checking, all saying at one and the same time with childish delight:

'Yes, of course, there's no doubt about it! Look! This one goes here, that one there and that one here, this one there.'

And the laughter of the adults mingled with the whistles of

the boys, the imprecations of the women, the old market gardener's tears of triumph and happiness and the shoves which the policemen were already giving to the proven thief, as if impatient to take him to prison.

There is no need to say that the policemen had that pleasure: that so-and-so was of course made to give the fifteen *duros* which he had received back to the stall-keeper; that the stall-keeper handed the money over at once to old Buscabeatas, and that the latter went back to Rota highly pleased, though he said as he went on his way:

'How lovely they looked in the market! I ought to have brought Manuela back to eat her tonight and keep the pips!'

November 1877

THE THREE-KEY BUGLE

You Can Do Anything You Really Want to Do

I

'PLAY the bugle, Don Basilio, and we'll dance! It isn't hot under these trees!'

'Yes, oh yes, Don Basilio, play the key-bugle!'

'Bring Don Basilio the bugle that Joaquín is learning on!'

'It's not much good. Will you play it, Don Basilio?'

'No!'

'What do you mean, no?'

'No, I won't!'

'Why not?'

'Because I don't know how.'

'Don't know how! What a hypocrite!'

'He must want us to pay to listen to him!'

'Come on! We know that you were a leading bandsman in the Infantry!'

'And that they listened to you at the Palace, when Espartero was in power.'

'And that you have a pension.'

'Come on, Don Basilio, give in!'

'Well now . . . yes, it's true. I have played the bugle. I was a . . . speciality act, as you call it now. But it's also a fact that I gave my bugle away two years ago to a poor discharged army bandsman and since then I haven't even . . . hummed a tune.'

'What a shame!'

'Another Rossini!'

'Ah! But this afternoon, you shall play!'

'Everything is allowed here in the country!'

'Remember it's my birthday, Grandpa!'

'Hurra! Hurra! Here's the bugle!'

'Yes, play!'

'A waltz!'

'No, a polka!'

'Polka? Get away with you! A fandango!'

'Yes, yes, a fandango, a Spanish dance!'

'I'm very sorry, my children, but I cannot play the bugle!'

'But you're always so nice.'

'So willing to please.'

'Your little grandson begs you!'

'And your niece!'

'Leave me alone, for God's sake. I've told you I won't play!'

'Why not?'

'Because I don't remember how and because, besides, I've sworn never to learn again.'

'Who did you swear to?'

'To myself, to a dead man, and, my daughter, to your poor mother!'

Everyone's face suddenly saddened when they heard those words.

'Oh! if you only knew at what expense I learnt to play the bugle,' added the old man.

'The story! The story!' exclaimed the young folk. 'Tell us the story!'

'Yes, it's true,' said Don Basilio, 'It's quite a tale. Listen to it and then you can judge whether or not I can play the bugle.'

And, sitting under a tree, surrounded by a group of curious and pleasant young people, he told the story of his music lessons.

In no dissimilar way did Mazeppa, Byron's hero, tell Charles XII one night, under another tree, the terrible stories of his horseriding lessons.

Let us listen to Don Basilio.

2

'Seventeen years ago civil war was raging here in Spain. Carlos and Isabel were disputing the crown and, divided into two camps, the Spanish people were spilling their blood in a fratricidal struggle.

'I had a friend, called Ramón Gámez. He was a Light Infantry lieutenant in my own battalion, the finest man I have ever known. We'd been brought up together, left school together, fought thousands of times together and together wished to die for freedom. I can honestly say that he was more Liberal than I and the whole army.

'But our commander committed a certain injustice in regard to Ramón, one of those abuses of authority which upset even the most honourable career. I mean to say that a piece of arbitrary behaviour made the Light Infantry lieutenant want to leave the ranks of his brothers, made the friend wish to leave his friend, the Liberal go over to the Carlist faction and the junior officer kill his Lieutenant-Colonel. Ramón wasn't the sort of person to put up with insults or injustice from anybody!

'Neither my threats, nor my supplications could dissuade him from his purpose. He had made up his mind! He would change his képi for the Carlist beret, even though he hated the rebels mortally.

'At that time we were in Catalonia, three leagues from the enemy.

'The night on which Ramón was to desert was rainy and cold, gloomy and sad, the eve of a battle.

'At about twelve Ramón entered my lodging.

'I was asleep.

' "Basilio," he whispered in my ear.

' "Who is it?"

' "It's me. Good-bye."

' "You're going now?"

' "Yes, *adiós*."

'And he took my hand:

' "Listen," he went on, "if there is a battle tomorrow, as they think there's going to be, and we meet during it . . ."

' "Yes, I know. We're friends."

' "Right. We embrace and then fight. I'll be killed tomorrow certainly, because I'm going to push aside everything in my way, until I kill the Lieutenant-Colonel. But,

Basilio, don't you risk your life. Glory disappears like a puff of smoke."

'"And, doesn't life?"

'"Yes, you're right. Become a major," exclaimed Ramón. "The pay isn't a puff of smoke except when you've smoked it all away. Oh, that's all over for me!"

'"What a depressing thought!" I said, not without some apprehension. "We'll both survive the battle tomorrow."

'"Well, let's fix a place to meet after it."

'"Where?"

'"At St Nicholas's shrine, at one o'clock in the morning. If either of us doesn't go, it'll be because he is dead. Agreed?"

'"Agreed."

'"Well then . . . *adiós!*"

'"*Adiós!*"

'Those were our words and, after an affectionate embrace, Ramón disappeared into the shadows of the night.

3

'As we expected, the rebels attacked us the next day.

'The battle was very bloody and lasted from three in the afternoon until nightfall.

'At about five o'clock, my battalion was energetically attacked by a force of Alavese led by Ramón.

'Ramón was already wearing the insignia of a major and the white Carlist beret!

'I ordered my men to fire at Ramón and Ramón ordered his to fire at me. That is, his men and my battalion fought hand-to-hand.

'We won in the end and Ramón had to flee with the very reduced remains of his Alavese, but not without first having personally killed, with a pistol shot, the man who the day before had been his Lieutenant-Colonel, who tried in vain to protect himself from his enemy's rage.

'At six o'clock the battle turned against us and part of my poor company and I were cut off and forced to surrender.

'So I was taken as a prisoner to the small town of — occupied by the Carlists since the beginning of that campaign and where they would presumably shoot me out of hand.

'There was no quarter given in war then.

4

'One o'clock in the morning of such an ominous day chimed, the time of my appointment with Ramón!

'I was imprisoned in a cell of the public gaol of that town.

'I asked about my friend and they answered:

' "He's very brave. He killed a Lieutenant-Colonel. But he must have died at the end of the battle."

' "What! Why do you say that?"

' "Because he hasn't returned from the field and the men who were under his orders today don't know anything of him."

'Ah! How terribly I suffered that night!

'One hope was left to me . . . that Ramón might be waiting for me at the shrine of St Nicholas and that for that reason he had not returned to the rebel camp.

' "How sad he will be when he sees that I don't keep our appointment," I thought. "He'll think I've been killed. And, am I in fact so far away from my last hour? The rebels always shoot their prisoners now, just as we do."

'So next morning dawned.

'A chaplain came into the prison.

'All my companions were asleep.

' "Death!" I exclaimed as I saw the priest.

' "Yes," he replied gently.

' "Now?"

' "No, within three hours."

'A minute later my companions were awake.

'Cries, sobs and blasphemies filled the prison air.

'Every man who is about to die usually takes hold of a certain idea and does not let go of it.

'Nightmare, fever or madness, this happened to me. The idea of Ramón, of Ramón alive, of Ramón dead, of Ramón in heaven, of Ramón at the shrine, gripped my brain with such force that I thought of nothing else during those agonizing hours.

'They removed my captain's uniform and put a cap and an old soldier's cloak on me.

'Thus I walked to death with my nineteen companions in misfortune.

'Only one had been reprieved . . . because of the coincidence of being a bandsman! At that time the Carlists granted bandsmen their lives as they were very short of them in their battalions.'

'And were you a bandsman, Don Basilio? Is that how you saved your life?' asked all the young people at once.

'No, my children,' replied the veteran, 'I was not a bandsman!

'They formed a square and placed us in the middle.

'I was number eleven, that is to say, I would be the eleventh to die.

'Then I thought of my wife and daughter, of you, my daughter and your mother!

'The shots began . . .

'Those explosions drove me mad.

'As my eyes were blindfolded, I did not see my companions fall.

'I tried to count the volleys, in order to know, a moment before dying, that my life in this world was ending.

'But I lost count after three or four.

'Oh! Those shots will thunder eternally in my heart and in my mind as they thundered that day!

'Now I thought I could hear them a thousand leagues away, then I felt them burst inside my head.

'And the firing went on.

'Now! I thought.

'And the volley cracked out, and I was alive.

'This is it! I said, finally.

'And I felt people grasping my shoulders, shaking me and shouting into my ear.

'I fell . . .

'I didn't think any more . . .

'But I felt as if I were deeply asleep . . .

'And I dreamt I had been shot.

6

'Then I dreamt that I was lying on a stretcher in my prison.

'I couldn't see.

'I put my hands to my eyes as if to remove a bandage and touched my open, wide-open eyes. Had I become blind?

'No. The prison was plunged in darkness.

'I heard the bells peal and I trembled.

'It was the sunset bell for the dead!

' "It's nine o'clock," I thought. "But on what day?"

'A shadow darker than the gloomy prison light bent over me.

'It appeared to be a man.

'And the rest? And the other eighteen?

'All had been shot!

'And I?

'I was alive, or in delirium inside the tomb.

'My lips automatically muttered a name, the ever-present name, my nightmare.

' "Ramón."

' "What is it?" replied the shadow beside me.

'I shuddered.

' "My God. Am I in the other world?"

' "No," said the same voice.

' "Ramón, are you alive?"

' "Yes."

' "And I."

' "Yes, alive also."

' "Where am I? Is this the shrine of St Nicholas? Aren't I a prisoner? Have I dreamt it all?"

' "No, Basilio, you haven't dreamed anything. Listen."

7

' "As you know, yesterday I killed the Lieutenant-Colonel in a fair fight. I have had my revenge! Then, maddened with rage, I went on killing and killing until after nightfall, until there wasn't a follower of Maria Cristina left on the battlefield.

' "When the moon rose, I thought of you. Then I made my way to the shrine of St Nicholas intending to wait for you.

' "It must have been about ten o'clock. Our appointment was for one, and I hadn't closed my eyes the previous night. So I fell into a deep sleep.

' "When the clock struck one I cried out and awoke.

' "I was dreaming that you were dead.

' "I looked around me and saw that I was alone.

' "What had happened to you?

' "The clock struck two, three, four o'clock. What a night of torment!

' "You didn't appear.

' "You must have been killed.

' "Dawn broke.

' "Then I left the shrine and came to this village to find the rebels.

' "I arrived as the sun was rising.

' "They all thought I had perished the day before.

' "So when they saw me they embraced me and the general heaped honours on me.

' "Then I learnt that twenty-one prisoners were going to be shot.

' "I had a sudden presentiment.

' "Can Basilio be one of them?" I said to myself.

' "So I ran to the place of execution.

' "The square was formed.

' "I heard some shots.

' "They had begun the executions.

' "I strained my eyes, but I couldn't see . . .

' "Pain blinded me, fear made me feel faint.

' "At last I spotted you.

' "You were about to be shot!

' "Two victims more and they would reach you.

' "What could I do?

' "I went mad. I cried out. I threw my arms around you and with a hoarse, broken, trembling voice, I exclaimed: 'Not this one, not this one, General!'

' "The general, who was commanding the firing-party and who knew me so well because of my conduct the previous day, asked me: 'Why not? Is he a bandsman, then?'

' "For me that word was like what suddenly seeing the sun in all its glory would be for a blind man.

' "The light of hope shone so brightly before my eyes that it blinded them.

' " 'A bandsman,' I exclaimed. 'Yes! Yes! General. He's a bandsman, a great bandsman!'

' "In the meanwhile you were lying there unconscious.

' " 'What instrument does he play?' asked the general.

' " 'The . . . er . . . the . . . er . . . the, yes, that's it, the keyed bugle!'

' " 'Do we need a bugler?' asked the general, turning to the band.

' "The answer took five seconds, five centuries, in coming.

' " 'Yes, General, we need one,' replied the bandmaster.

' " 'Right. Take that man out of the line and then go on with the executions,' exclaimed the Carlist leader.

' "Then I picked you up and brought you to this cell."

8

'Scarcely had Ramón finished, when I rose and said to him, with tears and laughter, embracing him and trembling: "I owe you my life!"

' "Not yet," answered Ramón.

' "What do you mean?" I exclaimed.

' "Can you play the bugle?"

' "No."

' "Then you don't owe me your life, but I have risked mine without saving yours."

'A sudden chill gripped me.

' "What about music?" asked Ramón. "Can you read it?"

' "Little, very little. You remember they taught us in school."

' "That's very little or rather nothing! You'll be shot. There's nothing to be done about it. You know that the band to which you'll belong will be organized in a fortnight!"

' "A fortnight!"

' "No more and no less! And, as you don't play the bugle – because God won't work a miracle – they'll shoot us both, no doubt of it."

' "Shoot you!" I exclaimed. "You! Because of me! Because of me and I owe you my life! Oh no! That can't be God's will. In a fortnight I shall be able to read music and I shall play the keyed bugle!"

'Ramón burst into laughter.

9

'What more do you want me to tell you, my children?

'In a fortnight – oh – will-power! – In fifteen days and fifteen nights (for I did not sleep or rest a moment in half a month) you may marvel at it, in a fortnight I learned to play the bugle!

'What days they were!

'Ramón and I would go out to the country and spend hours and hours with a certain musician who came every day from a near-by village to give me a lesson.

'*Escape*. I can read the word in your eyes. Oh! It was quite impossible! I was a prisoner and they kept watch over me. And Ramón did not wish to escape without me.

'And I didn't speak. I didn't think, I didn't eat.

'I was mad and my mania was music, the bugle, the damned keyed bugle.

'I wanted to learn and I learnt!

'And if I had been dumb, I should have learned to speak!

'Paralysed, I should have walked!

'And blind, I should have seen!

'Because I wanted to!

'Oh, will-power can do everything! If you wish it you can do it!

'I *wanted*, that is the great word!

'I *wanted*, and I succeeded. Children, learn this greatest of truths.

'So I saved my life and Ramón's.

'But I went mad.

'And, as a madman, my madness was my art.

'In three years the bugle never left my hand.

'Do-re-mi-fa-so-la-ti-, that was my world for all that time.

'My life was reduced to blowing.

'Ramón did not leave me.

'I emigrated to France and in France I went on playing the bugle.

'The bugle was me! I sang with the bugle to my lips!

'Men, villages, famous players gathered to hear me.

'It was a wonder, a marvel!

'The bugle bent in my hands, it became flexible, it groaned, wept, shouted, roared, imitated the birds, the beasts, and the sound of the human sob. My lungs were of brass.

'Two more years of that and then my friend died. As I looked at his body I recovered my reason.

'And when, fully sane again, I picked up the bugle one day, I was astonished to find that I couldn't play it.

'Now will you ask me to play music for you to dance to?'

Madrid, 1854

THE FOREIGNER

'STRENGTH does not consist in knocking one's enemy to the ground, but in overcoming one's own anger,' says an oriental maxim.

'Do not take advantage of your victory,' adds a book of our own religion.

'As for the guilty man who comes before you in judgement, consider him a miserable wretch, bound by the conditions of our depraved nature; and, in so far as it is in your power and without harming the other party, show yourself merciful and clement to him, for though the attributes of God are all equal, in our view, the attribute of pity shines brighter and stands out higher than that of justice.' This was Don Quixote's advice to Sancho Panza.

To illustrate all these most worthy teachings and to concede the demands of justice, we, who frequently take pleasure in recounting and rejoicing in the heroic deeds of the Spaniards during the Peninsular War, and in condemning and cursing the treachery and cruelty of the invaders, are today going to narrate a story which, though not weakening the love we have in our heart for our country, strengthens another feeling which is no less sublime and profoundly Christian: love for one's neighbour. Because of the congenital misfortune of the human race, that feeling must come to terms with the harsh laws of war, but it can and must shine out when the enemy is humiliated.

2

'Good day, old man,' I said.

'God keep you, Señorito,' he replied.

'You're very much alone along these roads.'

'Yes, Señor. I've come from the mines at Linares, where I've been working for a few months, and I'm going to Gádor to see my family. You'll be going to . . . ?'

'I'm going to Almería and I've walked ahead of the wagon a little because I like to enjoy these beautiful April mornings. But, if I'm not mistaken, you were praying when I arrived. Please don't let me stop you. I'll go on reading meanwhile, since that wretched wagon is so slow that one can study in the middle of the road.'

'Come now! That book is some story or other. And who told you that I was praying?'

'Well! I saw you take your hat off and cross yourself.'

'What the devil! I mean . . . why should I deny it? Yes, I was praying. Everybody's got his accounts to settle with God.'

'That's very true!'

'Do you intend to walk for a long way?'

'Me? As far as the inn.'

'In that case, go down that path and we'll take a short cut.'

'With pleasure. That looks like a very pleasant little valley. Let's go down there.'

And, following the old man, I shut my book, left the road and made my way down to a picturesque ravine.

The green tints and the diaphanous distant horizon, as well as the line of the mountains, indicated already that the Mediterranean was not far away.

For a few minutes we walked in silence until the old miner suddenly stopped.

'Exactly!' he exclaimed.

And once more he took off his hat and crossed himself.

We were under some fig trees already heavy with leaves, and by the side of a fast-running stream.

'Now, come on, Grandpa,' I said as I sat down on the grass. 'Tell me what happened here.'

'What! You know?' he said, shuddering.

'All I know,' I added with great calm, 'is that a man died here . . . and a nasty death from all appearances!'

'You're not wrong, Señorito, you're not wrong! But who told you . . .?'

'I know from your prayers.'

'That's very true. That's why I am praying.'

I looked at the miner's face carefully and realized that he had always been an honourable man. He was not far from weeping and his praying was tranquil and gentle.

'Sit down here, friend,' I said, handing him a cigarette.

'Well, I'll tell you, Señorito. Oh! Thanks very much! It's very thin!'

'Join two together and you'll get a thick one,' I added, giving him another cigarette.

'Bless you! Well Señor,' said the old man, sitting down beside me, 'forty-five years ago on a morning very like this, I was walking down here at almost the same time.'

'Forty-five years,' I thought.

And the weight of time past fell on my spirit. Where had all the flowers of those forty-five springs gone? The snow of seventy winters whitened the forehead of the old man.

When he saw that I said nothing, he lit tinder, then lit his cigarette and continued in these words:

'It's pretty weak stuff, this tobacco! Well, Señor, on the day I was telling you about. I was coming from Gérgal with a load of saltwort and when I arrived at the spot where we left the road and came along this path, I met two Spanish soldiers with a Polish prisoner. That was the time when the first French were here, not the ones who came in 1823, but the others . . .'

'Yes, I understand. You're talking about the War of Independence.'

'Oh, you hadn't even been born then!'

'I should say not!'

'Oh, of course. I suppose it's down in that book you were

reading. But, you know, those books never tell you the best things about these wars. They write what suits them . . . and people believe it without question. It's obvious. You've got to be threescore and ten years old, as I'll be come June, to know a few things. Anyway, that Pole was in Napoleon's army, Napoleon, the villain who's died already . . . because the priest says there's another . . . But I don't think this one will come to these parts. What do you think, Señorito?'

'What can I say?'

'Yes, of course! You won't have learnt about those things yet, sir. Oh! His Reverence, who's very well educated, knows when the Mamelukes will come to an end in the East and the Russians and Muscovites will come to Gádor and take away the Constitution. Still, I'll be dead by then! So, I'll go back to the story of my Pole.

'The poor man had been left sick at Fiñana, while his comrades retreated towards Almería. He had fever, as I learnt later. An old woman was looking after him out of charity, caring little that he was an enemy. (That little old woman must have enjoyed many years of Paradise now for that good deed!) She kept him hidden in her cellar, near the castle.

'And that is where, the previous night, two Spanish soldiers who were on their way to rejoin their battalion, and, as luck would have it, went in to light a cigar from the lamp in that solitary dwelling, discovered the poor Pole. Lying in a corner, he was uttering words in his language in the delirium of fever.

' "Let's hand him over to our officer!" said the Spaniards to each other. "The bastard'll be shot tomorrow and we'll be promoted."

'Iwa, which was the Pole's name, as the old woman told me later, had been ill with intermittent fever for six months already and was very weak, very thin and almost consumptive.

'The good woman wept and begged, protesting that the foreigner could not possibly begin a journey without falling down dead in half an hour.

'But the only result was that they knocked her about for

her lack of "patriotism". I still haven't forgotten that word which I had never heard uttered before!

'As for the Pole, you can imagine what the state of his mind was. He was flat on his back with fever and the few odd half-Polish, half-Spanish words which came from his lips made the two soldiers laugh.

' "Shut up, *Parlyvoo*, Pig, Frog!" said they.

'And they struck him till he got up from his bed.

'So as not to weary you, Señorito, in that state, half-naked, hungry, stumbling, dying, the poor man walked five leagues!

'Five leagues, Señor. Do you know how many steps there are in five leagues? Well, it's from Fiñana to here. . . and on foot! Barefoot!

'Just think of it! A delicate man, a handsome young chap, as fair as a woman, sick, after six months intermittent fever, and suffering from an attack of it just then!'

'How could he stick it out?'

'Ah! He didn't!'

'But how did he walk five leagues?'

'How? Pricked on with bayonet stabs!'

'Go on, old man, go on.'

'I was coming along this ravine, as usual, to save a little walking, and they were walking up there on the road. So I stopped, just here, to watch the end of that horror, while I pretended to roll a black cigar, the sort we had then.

'Iwa was panting like a dog about to have a fit of rabies. His head was bare, he was as yellow as a dug-up corpse, with two scarlet patches high up on his cheeks and his eyes bright and dull at the same time . . . in other words, like Christ on his way to Calvary.

' "I want to die! Kill me, for God's sake!" stammered the foreigner, his hands clasped in supplication.

'The Spaniards laughed at his ramblings and called him *Frenchy*, *Parlyvoo* and other things.

'At last Iwa's legs collapsed under him and he fell flat on the ground. I breathed a sigh of relief, for I thought the poor fellow had given up the ghost.

'But a bayonet stab in the shoulder made him stand up again.

'Then he made for this ridge to hurl himself over it and thus die.

'The soldiers prevented him because it didn't suit them that their prisoner should die. They saw me here with my mule, which, as I have said, was loaded with saltwort.

' "Oy! Mate!" they said to me, pointing their rifles at me, "Bring that mule up here!'

'I obeyed without protest, thinking I was helping the foreigner.

' "Where are you going?" they asked when I had climbed up.

' "I'm going to Almería," I answered, "and what you're doing is inhuman!"

' "None of your sermons!" shouted one of the torturers.

' "A Frenchified muleteer!" exclaimed the other.

' "Talk too much and you'll see what'll happen to you!"

'A rifle butt struck my chest.

'It was the first time that any man, except my father, had ever hit me!

' "No irritate, no make trouble!" exclaimed the Pole, grasping my feet, for he had fallen to the ground once more.

' "Unload the saltwort," said the soldiers to me.

' "What for?"

' "To load this bastard on the mule."

' "That's different. I'll do it with great pleasure."

'Having said that I began to unload.

' "No, no, no!" exclaimed Iwa, "You let them kill me."

' "I don't want them to kill you, poor chap!" I exclaimed as I clasped the young man's burning hands.

' "But I yes want! Kill you me, for God's sake!"

' "You want me to kill you?'

' "Yes . . . yes . . . good man, suffer much!"

'My eyes filled with tears.

'I turned to the soldiers and said to them in a voice which would have melted a stone:

' "Spaniards, compatriots, brothers! Another Spaniard,

who loves our country as much as any man begs you . . . leave me alone with this man!"

' "I said he was Frenchified," exclaimed one of them.

' "Confounded muleteer," said the other, "careful what you say or I'll break your head."

' "Damned soldier!" I answered with equal force. "I'm not afraid of dying. You're two heartless wretches. You're two strong armed men against a helpless dying man. You're cowards! Give me one of those rifles and I'll fight with you until I kill you or die myself, but leave this poor, sick man alone. He can't defend himself."

'Oh, I went on, seeing that one of those beasts was blushing with shame: "if you have children as I have, if you think that tomorrow they might be in the homeland of this unfortunate man, in the same situation as he is now, alone, dying, far from their parents; if you think that this Pole doesn't even know what he's doing in Spain, that he's probably a conscript snatched away from his family to serve the ambition of a king . . . what the devil! You would pardon him. Yes! because you are men before being Spaniards, and this Pole is a man, a brother of yours. What will Spain profit from the death of a man afflicted with fever? Fight to the death with all Napoleon's grenadiers, but let it be on the battlefield. And pardon the weak, be generous with the defeated! Be Christians, do not be executioners!"

' "That's enough sermonizing!" said the soldier who had always led in their cruel actions, the one who had forced Iwa to walk by stabbing him with a bayonet, the one who wanted to buy a promotion for the price of Iwa's body.

' "What shall we do, mate?" asked the other, somewhat moved by my words.

' "Quite simple," the first answered, "Look!"

'And without giving me time to foresee, let alone impede his movements, he fired a shot into Iwa's heart.

'Iwa looked at me gratefully, whether before or after dying I could not say.

'His look promised me heaven, where perhaps the martyr was already.

'Then the two soldiers beat me up with the ramrods of their rifles.

'The one who had killed the foreigner cut off one of his ears and put it in his pocket.

'It was the testimonial for the promotion he wanted!

'Then he stripped Iwa and robbed him . . . even of a certain medallion (with a picture of a woman or a saint) which he wore around his neck.

'Then they went off towards Almería.

'I buried Iwa in this ravine, there, where you are sitting and went back to Gérgal, because I knew I was ill.

'And true enough, that adventure made me seriously ill, bringing me almost to the doors of death.'

'And didn't you see those two soldiers again? Don't you know their names?'

'No, Señor, but, from the details that the old woman who had looked after the Pole gave me later, I learned that one of the two Spaniards was nicknamed 'Laughs' and he was precisely the one who had murdered and robbed the poor foreigner.'

At this point the wagon caught up with us. The old man and I climbed up to the road. We shook hands and said good-bye, happy to have known each other. We had wept together!

3

Three nights afterwards, several friends and I were having coffee in Almería's delightful gentlemen's club.

Near us at another table were two old men, retired officers; one a major and the other a colonel, as we were informed by somebody who knew them.

We could hear what they were saying in spite of ourselves, for they spoke very loudly, as is customary in people who have been accustomed to command.

Suddenly my ears were struck and my attention drawn by a sentence of the Colonel's:

'Poor Laughs . . .'.

'Laughs,' I exclaimed inwardly. And I began to listen intently.

'Poor Laughs,' the Colonel said, 'was captured by the French when they took Málaga and, taken from depot to depot, he ended up in Switzerland of all places, where I was also a prisoner, like all of us who couldn't escape with the Marquess of La Romana. I met him there, because he became friendly with Juan, the servant I have had all my life, or all my career. When Napoleon was so cruel as to take all the Spanish prisoners in his power to Russia as part of his Grande Armée I took Laughs as my orderly. Then I learnt that he had an uncontrollable fear of the Poles, or a superstitious terror of Poland, because he did nothing but ask Juan and me if "we would have to pass through that country to reach Russia", shuddering at the thought that such might be the case. Doubtless, that man, whose head was not very strong because he had abused it so much with spiritous liquors but who otherwise was a good soldier and a fair cook, had had serious trouble with some Pole, whether in the war in Spain or in his long pilgrimage through other countries. We arrived in Warsaw, where we stopped for some days. Laughs fell seriously ill with brain fever as a result of the panic which had gripped him as soon as we set foot on Polish soil. I had a certain affection for him and did not want to leave him there alone when we received the order to march, so I got my superiors to agree to Juan's staying in Warsaw to look after him. He also had orders that, once the illness ended in one way or another, he was to catch up with me in one of the many convoys of equipment or supplies which followed the enormous mass of men of which my regiment was in the vanguard. You can just imagine my surprise when, the same day as we started out and only a few hours after beginning our march, my ex-servant, terrified out of his wits, reported to me and told me what had just happened to poor Laughs. I can tell you that it is one of the most extraordinary and mystifying cases that has ever happened. Listen to me and you'll see that I have had good reason not to forget the story in forty-two years.

' Juan had found a good lodging to look after Laughs, in

the house of a widow of a farmer, with three daughters of marriageable age. Since we Spaniards had reached Warsaw, she had never stopped asking several of us, through French interpreters, if we knew anything of a son of hers, called Iwa, who went to fight in Spain in 1808 and of whom she had had no news for three years, something which was not the case with other families in the same situation. As Juan was such a flatterer, he found a way of consoling and giving hope to that sad mother. That is why, in return, she offered to care for Laughs when he fell ill with brain fever in her presence. They arrived at the good woman's house and, when she was helping to undress the sick man, Juan suddenly saw her grow pale and convulsively grip a certain silver medallion, with an effigy or portrait in miniature, which Laughs always wore on his chest under his clothes as a sort of talisman or spell against the Poles, thinking that it represented a Virgin or Saint of that country.

' "Iwa! Iwa!" cried the widow in a horrifying voice, shaking the sick man, who understood nothing as he was in a coma from the fever. At her cries her daughters came, and, informed of what had happened, they took the medallion, held it beside their mother's face, indicating to Juan by means of signs that he should see, as he did, that the effigy was in fact the portrait of that woman. Then they turned to him, and, seeing that his compatriot could not answer them, began to ask him a large number of questions in words unintelligible to him, but with gestures and attitudes which gave evidence of the most frightening rage. Juan shrugged his shoulders, giving them to understand by signs that he knew nothing of where the medallion had come from and that he had known Laughs for a very short time. The noble face of my most honest servant must have proved to those four infuriated lionesses that the poor fellow was not to blame. Besides, he hadn't been wearing the portrait! But the other one! They killed the other one, poor Laughs, by beating him to death and then tearing him to pieces with their nails! That's all I know about the drama, because I've never been able to discover why Laughs had that picture.'

'Allow me to tell you why,' I said, unable to restrain myself.

And, going up to the Colonel and the Major at their table I was introduced to them by my friends and told them the entire hair-raising tale that the miner had told me.

When I had finished, the Major, a man of more than seventy, exclaimed with the simple faith of an old soldier, with the impulsiveness of a good Spaniard and all the authority of his white hair:

'By God, gentlemen, there's more in all this than simple coincidence!'

Almería, 1854